THE
STEPHEN
HAWKING
DEATH ROW FAN CLUB

THE
STEPHEN HAWKING
DEATH ROW FAN CLUB

Six Stories and a Novella

R.C. GOODWIN

LANGDON STREET PRESS
MINNEAPOLIS

Langdon Street Press
322 First Avenue N, 5th floor
Minneapolis, MN 55401
612.455.2293
www.langdonstreetpress.com

ISBN-13: 978-1-63413-015-8
LCCN: 2014948831

Distributed by Itasca Books

Cover Design by Alan Pranke
Typeset by Mary Kristin Ross
Edited by Robert Christian Schmidt

Printed in the United States of America

LANGDON
STREET
PRESS

CONTENTS

BLANK SLATE

RAY HAZEN WAS ONE OF THE MOST DANGEROUS AND UNPREDICTABLE INMATES IN NEW ENGLAND, a fact belied by his short stature and slender build. At five foot eight, he weighed only 160. Horn-rimmed glasses and a receding chin added to the look of harmlessness.

His original offenses had been relatively minor, two counts of possession with intent to sell and a second-degree assault. He received a four-year sentence, suspended after two—shorter than it might have been. The judge sent him to a Level Two facility. Minimum security.

Ray's youth had prompted leniency. Barely nineteen, he made a good impression in the courtroom. He spoke courteously to the judge: "Yes, Your Honor . . . No, Your Honor . . . All I want is for people to give me another chance . . ." He showed no anger when the prosecutor

1

tried to bait him on cross-examination. His brown hair was neatly trimmed, and he'd shaved off his scruffy beard and Fu Manchu mustache. Wearing khakis and a white shirt under a blue pullover, he looked more collegiate than criminal.

The clothes concealed tattoos that might have made the judge less sympathetic—a swastika and a caricatured black man, thick-lipped with bulging eyes, about to be hanged by Klansmen. Also a *Heil Hitler!* misspelled as *Hile.* While still in a juvenile facility, he'd joined the Aryan Ramblers, a white power gang notorious for intimidating nonmembers, on whom they were quick to mete out casual and ruthless bloodshed. Insulting one, intentionally or otherwise, could land you in the hospital.

The man Ray had assaulted, Danny Lloyd Jeffries— as disheveled and surly as Ray was well groomed and polite—did not evoke much sympathy. Danny Lloyd's rap sheet listed convictions for dealing, burglary, carjacking and domestic violence. He'd spent twelve of his thirty-two years behind bars.

There was also a question of who'd started things. "I was only trying to defend myself," Ray testified, allowing just the right degree of fear to come into his tone. "He would have killed me if he had the chance."

Ray remained more sympathetic than Danny Lloyd, even when it came out that he'd broken the older man's jaw and cheekbone with a beer bottle and then kneed him in the crotch for good measure.

Ray's time served might have been even shorter, as little as eighteen months if he behaved. Instead, his sentence swelled to almost twenty years.

By the time he had served six months, he'd received twenty-eight disciplinary write-ups. His infractions ranged from fighting to making *pruno* in his cell—a distilled concoction with the smoothness and subtlety of paint remover. He routinely hurled threats and obscenities at Correctional Officers (COs). He spent four of those first six months in restrictive housing, punitive segregation, or "seg." In one fight, he bit off part of another inmate's ear. New charges added eight more years to his sentence. This time, the judge was unmoved by his youth and Joe College appearance.

By the time he served a year, he'd been in two more fights. They'd also caught him forcing another inmate to fellate him in a stairwell—"Listen, douche bag, I'll break your neck if you don't do what I tell you to. And that's *after* I break three or four of your fingers." The COs often searched his cell for contraband and almost always found it. Weapons—a shiv, and a dagger made from a melted toothbrush. Marijuana, Valium and Vicodin smuggled from outside. Money extorted from other inmates. They added ten more years to his sentence; they also transferred him to Orrington, the state's Level Five facility. Maximum security.

The Orrington philosophy, as espoused by the warden, Gary Gunther, was the gist of his speech to every new CO. The speech went like this: "They're here because society must be protected from them and no other place can deal with them, not even another prison. We aren't interested in their rehabilitation, their mental health or their shitty little souls. They come here with essentially no privileges, which will be granted, very gradually, if they keep their noses clean and make no trouble. If they break rules, if they so much as pass gas without permission, they'll receive harsh and immediate punishment. Judges and lawyers can't protect them."

Orrington housed the most violent of the violent, the attackers of COs and other inmates, the high-profile gang bangers and the state's few death row prisoners. Notwithstanding the violence and malice of his fellow prisoners, Ray still attained a special status. He kicked one CO in the ankle, an injury serious enough to require surgery, and threw a mixture of urine and feces in another's face.

Punishment at Orrington meant an inmate might be held in four-point restraints against a bare bed frame. He might be maced, or pummeled with a phonebook, which left few marks. None of this had much effect on Ray, except to add to his reservoir of rage.

Apart from his reputation, which Ray did his best to cultivate, there was also the matter of *the look*. He had unnerving pale blue eyes, and no one could outstare him. At best, the look expressed dismissal; at worst, a resolve to destroy you. And the look conveyed a defiant challenge: "Do your worst. You will not break me."

Orrington inmates had access to mental health services, and Ray occasionally requested them. Every three months or so, he met with Duane Case, the prison's senior social worker. Less frequently, once or twice a year, he met with Herbert Valentine, the psychiatrist. These visits tended to be brief. Valentine, an African-American, had limited tolerance for Ray's racism.

Ray's meetings with Case followed a set pattern. Case asked how he was doing, and Ray launched into a diatribe about COs who tormented him, and how someone should tell the miserable bastards that cruel and unusual punishment is unconstitutional, and how blacks and Latinos should be lined up and shot, and how Hitler had the right ideas except he didn't go far enough. After that came Ray's standard demand for meds. "Why doncha do something useful for a change and tell Valentine to get off his lazy fat black ass and give me something for my nerves and back pain? Xanax and Percodans would be good." Case explained, again, that Valentine would never prescribe addictive medications for vague symptoms but he might prescribe something to stabilize Ray's moods and manage his outbursts. At this point, Ray typically lambasted him as a useless jerk-off and demanded to be taken back to his cell, where at least he had peace and quiet, and he wouldn't waste time talking to some asshole of a social worker.

Unsurprisingly, Ray made enemies of a number of nonwhite inmates. He never kept his racist views secret.

Some of the Orrington inmates did keep out of trouble, and they slowly gained a few privileges, such as the chance to attend vocational classes and twelve-step meetings. But Ray never made it off A-Block, the most restricted unit. Those on A-Block stayed in their cells except for thrice-weekly showers, closely scrutinized visits, sick call and half an hour of recreation (rec) each day if they'd caused no recent problems. Rec meant walking outside in groups of five or six on a concrete patio surrounded by razor-tipped barbed wire. Still, as limited as it was, the A-Block population cherished it. It gave them a chance to leave their cells and talk to other inmates. This was hard to do otherwise, since the unit consisted of single cells and they didn't eat communally. It also let them see the sky.

One early April afternoon, halfway through his third year there, Ray left his cell for rec. His group consisted of five other inmates: two blacks, two Latinos and another white. The warm bright day hinted of the coming summer. Ray walked alone, ignoring the other white guy's efforts to strike up conversation. In a flash the blacks and Latinos were all over him, landing punches to his head and gut. Once they had him down, punches turned to kicks. Before the COs broke it up, he sustained three separate fractures to his skull. His assailants also broke his nose and six ribs and knocked out a handful of his teeth. One of them had landed full force on his right knee; his lower leg stuck outward, almost at a right angle to his thigh. It happened in seconds, and Ray never knew what hit him.

Inmate violence, as a rule, is too commonplace to be newsworthy unless it turns into a riot. But the attack on Ray got into a few papers, and one TV station mentioned it. Its brutality went well beyond the usual.

*   *   *

No one expected him to live. He had extensive internal injuries as well as the fractured skull. Surgeons drained a quart and a half of blood from his abdomen; they also took out his spleen and hopelessly damaged left kidney. His twice-ruptured colon necessitated a temporary colostomy. Separate surgical teams tended to his brain, his abdomen and his shattered knee. In all, they kept him in the OR for more than seven hours.

Over the course of the next few days, it appeared possible—and then likely—that he'd survive, but the quality of his survival was anybody's guess. Some of his doctors predicted a persistent vegetative state. The more optimistic ones predicted that he'd regain consciousness but wouldn't walk or talk or care for himself in a meaningful way. He'd have to be taught to do everything again.

The optimistic ones proved right. Three weeks after the attack, Ray regained consciousness. Four weeks after that, he was transferred to a hospital specializing in long-term rehabilitation.

In time, he could sit up in bed, and then get out of bed and sit in a chair. He began to feed himself, which meant holding a cup, glass, straw or spoon—he was still on a liquid and pureed diet. After the removal of his catheter and reversal of his colostomy, he learned to tend to his bodily functions. Step by step he learned to walk again, first with a walker and then a cane, and finally unaided. Mastering each task became a colossal undertaking: the ability to wash his face or blow his nose, to put on underwear, to add milk and sugar to a bowl of oatmeal.

At first he uttered no more than grunts and groans, but word by word his vocabulary came back to him. He learned to ask for applesauce and chocolate milk, his favorite food and drink (because of his slurred speech and missing teeth, he called them *appuhsau* and *shacamill*). He learned to address his nurses and physical therapists by name, and to ask for a robe if the room got too cold.

He became the doctors' and nurses' prize patient, in large part because of his miraculous progress. Furthermore, the new Ray was pleasant and appreciative, like a little boy relishing the attention of his caretakers. He always said *please*, a word he'd never used before the beating, and nodded his thanks when others helped him.

Recollections of his early life proved vague and spotty. "I used to live near a lake," he told a nurse. It was true; he'd grown up in Vermont, on the shores of Lake

Champlain. "Mom smoked and Dad had a big brown beard," he went on. "'Cept for a coupla things like that, it's pretty much a blank." His amnesia might have been a blessing. Both parents, abusive alcoholics, had dished out punishments like locking him in a closet all day or throwing him down a flight of stairs. They divorced when he was ten. His mother died in a car crash a year later, his father died of cirrhosis a year after that. An older sister ran away at seventeen and no one heard from her again. A younger brother was serving fifteen to twenty in a Vermont prison.

While aware that he came from Orrington, the people around him knew few details of his criminal background. An exception was an African-American nurse named Barbara Blaine. Barbara's brother worked as an Orrington CO, and he told her stories of Ray's unprovoked attacks and racism. She was therefore less enamored with him than her colleagues, tending to him with a frosty efficiency, speaking to him only when she had to.

One evening, Ray practiced walking in the corridor, his gait slow and wobbly as usual. His injured knee gave way and he came crashing down, landing on his shoulder and elbow. He cried out, and Barbara came to his assistance. She helped him up without a word or hint of empathy and steered him back to bed.

As she turned to leave his room, he turned to her. "Barbara?"

"What."

"How come you don't talk to me?"

"I do talk to you. I'm talking to you now."

"Not the way the others do." A schoolboy, wounded by rejection. "Why don't you like me?"

Nonplussed, she didn't know how to answer him. She thought it unfair to blame Ray for things he'd done before, especially since he had no memory of them; he was barely the same person. Still, she found it hard to let go of his past. Every time she saw Ray's collection of tattoos, she wished he'd died.

"You used to do a lot of bad stuff," she said finally.

"What kind of bad stuff?"

Barbara sauntered to his bedside chair. "You used to be very angry. Especially with people who . . . didn't look like you. People with darker skins. Any chance you got, you tried to hurt them."

"Why would I do things like that?"

"No one can answer that but you, Ray." She felt a softening towards him in spite of herself, and in spite of a deep skepticism. For all she knew he remained a hardcore racist beneath the simpleminded charm. But had he? The man-child on the bed seemed genuinely likeable. It confused her.

"Rosie and Junior are real good to me," Ray went on. "They take care of me and talk to me, they make me laugh." Rosie Oviedo was a mixed-race nurse from the Dominican Republic; Junior Wiggins was a black physical therapist. "I like 'em. I don't want *anybody* hurting 'em."

Barbara had no idea what to make of this.

They brought him picture books, and reacquainted him with the alphabet, teaching him to read and write again. Like a Talmudic scholar poring over ancient texts, he struggled with simple sentences. *The dog barked. She fed the cat.* They walked with him on the hospital grounds, throwing around a tennis ball with him. At first, his throws were feeble and off the mark, but slowly his strength and aim improved. Nurses brought in treats, plates of chocolate chip cookies and homemade fudge, ramekins of rice pudding. Even Barbara contributed, bringing him a slab of sweet potato pie. He met these acts with unfailing gratitude and politeness.

By late October, he was ready to leave the hospital. Bureaucrats debated what to do with him; deliberations reached the governor. Ray's caretakers held that he should go to a Level Two facility. They argued that he posed no risk to anyone now, and a Level Two would allow him to get the medical attention he still needed, especially physical and speech therapy.

People in Corrections took a harder line. Ray had committed dozens of violent acts before and after his arrest, and he deserved punishment for them; that was the gist of it. And who could *really* say he wouldn't do those things again? They believed the Ray they knew and feared would reappear, sooner or later. Representatives of the COs' union took a particularly hard line, since they stood to lose the most when he regressed. "Rattlesnakes don't change their colors," said one of them sagely.

In the end the hardliners won, and Ray went back to Orrington.

*   *   *

Warden Gunther called a special meeting the morning of Ray's homecoming. He opened with some off-the-cuff remarks. He knew Ray's return had sparked controversy, but he believed they made the right decision. "Doctors and nurses meant well," he said with a glance towards Valentine, "but they could be naïve when it came to the likes of *Mr. Hazen*"—Gunther pronounced the words with exaggerated mock respect. "At Orrington you see people as they are, not as you want them to be. Your life depends on it. Twenty years in Corrections has taught me something about behavior. I know a man beyond redemption when I see one, and *Mr. Hazen* is one of them."

Valentine addressed the group next. He admitted that he lacked the Warden's depth of experience since he'd only worked in Corrections fifteen years himself. "Besides," he went on, I don't know who's beyond redemption or who isn't; I don't have such God-like wisdom. But I do know a bit about traumatic brain injury and the profound, mysterious changes that can result from it. I urge you to be open to the possibility that Ray *might* have become a different man from the one you're all familiar with." As he talked, a few attendees rolled their eyes, a few yawned.

Several other COs spoke. They recounted stories of Ray's brutality and explosiveness. The unnerving way he had of looking fairly human one minute and turning into a rabid dog the next. One of them suggested that the inmates who attacked him should have been rewarded, maybe with a year or two knocked off their sentences. Another theorized that Ray remained as violent as always but possessed enough shrewdness to feign amnesia, bide his time and put on an act until he might catch them off guard. "I'm just sayin', that's when he could *really* do some harm."

On only one point did the administration cut Ray any slack. He'd be housed in Orrington's small hospital wing instead of A-Block. Gunther reluctantly agreed that Ray would need special care, and he could best receive it there. Being in the hospital wing would also keep him relatively safe from other inmates, many of whom wished he'd died.

Among those present at the meeting was Lieutenant Eduardo Lorca, the CO at whom Ray had thrown feces and urine. Ray had no particular animus towards Lorca, who merely walked by his cell in the course of one of his frequent bad days.

Lorca, a fastidious man, found himself haunted by the incident. Recollections of the smell, warmth and feel of the mixture ambushed him at random as he drove to work, watched the late news or had pizza with his family. Sometimes he woke in the middle of the night and they were powerful enough to bring him close to vomiting. He'd wash his face for five or ten minutes. By then he found it impossible to fall asleep again.

Lorca had waited eagerly for Ray's return.

*   *   *

Ray's new home in the hospital wing consisted of a tiny cell with gray cinderblock walls, a narrow bed, a metal sink and toilet, and a stool and table bolted to the floor. A single bulb, encased in steel mesh lest an occupant break it and use the pieces as weapons, provided light. The rectangular window, a foot wide and three feet high, afforded the only view outside. Unlike his window at the rehab hospital, this one could not be opened.

Besides his clothing and few toiletries, Ray's only possessions were some picture books, coloring books and crayons, arranged neatly on the table.

The Orrington nurses and aides, in contrast to his previous caretakers, knew the old Ray, the one who hit or spat at them if they looked at him cross-eyed, who rejected every human overture. Stolid in the face of his friendliness, they weren't about to spend an unnecessary minute with him. Here he'd get no reading lessons, no homemade cookies.

Their manner left Ray sad and mystified. Sometimes it made him cry. When he did, they made fun of him. *What's the matter, widdle boy, is someone being mean to you?* He learned not to cry, at least in front of others.

Shortly after Ray's transfer back to Orrington, Case visited him in the hospital's glass-walled day room. Since Ray had no memory of him, Case reintroduced himself. Ray's blue eyes, duller than Case remembered, conveyed distrust and uncertainty. He didn't know what to expect from others now, if they'd be nice like the ones at rehab or not-nice like most of the ones here. At least Case smiled, so Ray thought he might be one of the nice ones.

"I don't like this place," he told Case.

"Why is that, Ray?"

Ray leaned towards Case. "I miss the other ones. Junior and Sharon and Eddie and Rosie and the rest of 'em. They treated me good. These ones here won't even talk to me."

"You haven't been here very long. Maybe they'll treat you better once they get to know you."

He looked at Case pleadingly. "Can't you send me back to the other place?"

"I wish I could, but people decided that this is where you need to be now."

"What people?"

"People who run the prisons . . . who remember how you used to be. You'll have to show them you're different."

Ray stood up and paced. "I wanna know more about what was I like before."

Case wondered how open he should be. "Sometimes you lost your temper," he answered ambiguously. "Sometimes you yelled or threw things. Or got into fights."

"I don't remember that. I still don't remember much of anything. But I'll show 'em," vowed Ray. "I'll show 'em I'm real good now."

"That's the best thing for you to do," said Case, wondering how much difference it would make.

The next day, Eduardo Lorca came to see Ray in his cell. Sitting on the stool, Ray greeted him with his crooked smile and said hello. He offered his hand to the stranger. People liked that, he'd learned, at least sometimes. Ignoring the outstretched hand, Lorca made no response at all. He stood over Ray, arms akimbo.

"Hello," Ray tried again. *Hawwo,* the word came out. His injuries and missing teeth still affected his pronunciation. Again, he got no answer.

"My name is Lieutenant Lorca," he said eventually. "You do not remember me, I guess."

"No."

In a single fluid motion Lorca reached out and

slapped Ray across the mouth, hard enough to make his lip bleed. Ray flinched and rubbed his face.

"No, *Sir*. You will always call me *Sir*. And you will stand up when we are together."

Ray continued to rub his face. "Does that mean you want me to stand up now?"

"'Do you want me to stand up now, *Sir*?'" Lorca corrected him. Another slap, this one across the bridge of Ray's nose. "Yes, I do. Here, I'll help you." He pulled Ray up by an ear.

Ray wanted to cry out. His face stung, his ear hurt, and his nose as well as his lip was bleeding, but something told him not to. He knew instinctively that crying out would make things worse. Instead, he stood between the stool and the bed, hands dangling, saying nothing, waiting. Lorca waited too. From time to time the CO touched his tongue to his upper teeth, very quickly, almost imperceptibly.

"I will come to see you often," Lorca said. "Sometimes twice a week and sometimes twice a day. It will vary. When I do, you will do exactly what I say. You will stand until I tell you to sit down, which I probably won't. You will not speak unless you are spoken to. You will follow every rule to the letter." Ray didn't know what *to the letter* meant but thought it best to nod anyway.

Lorca walked around the cell, inspecting it inch by inch, ripping sheets and blanket from the mattress, poking the pillow. He paid particular attention to the objects on Ray's table. Pointing to the books, he asked, "Who gave you these?"

"Sharon and Rosie . . . *Sir*. To help me learn to read and write again."

"You are not allowed to have unauthorized reading material. Nor are you allowed to have crayons and pencils without special permission."

Ray looked at him, perplexed. For one thing, he didn't understand a lot of what the man was saying: *unauthorized . . . without special permission*. More importantly, no one had treated him this way since he'd regained consciousness. "But I can't learn to read and write again without them—"

Lorca hooked a foot around Ray's ankle and knocked him off his feet. Ray fell into a heap, too surprised to make a sound. "'But I can't learn to read and write again without them, *Sir*,'" Lorca corrected him. About to leave, he picked up the crayons, books and pencils. "One other thing. What happens between us concerns no one else. Keep it to yourself or I will kill you."

*   *   *

"I don't know what's going on with Ray, but I don't like it," Case said as he sat in Valentine's office. "He only came back here three weeks ago and he's already completely different."

"How so?"

"For one thing, he was friendly. He'd chatter on and on. He'd smile from time to time, and sometimes he even joked with me. Now it's a struggle to get ten words from him. When he does talk, it's mostly about the other place, as he calls it. How nice the people were, and could I help him get back there—"

"Can you blame the poor bastard? What would *you* prefer, being there or in this hell-hole? Rehab was probably the only place where they treated him halfway decently. He must miss them something fierce."

"I'm sure he does, but there's something else. I think the COs are pretty rough on him. Maybe the hospital staff, too. A couple of times I've noticed some bruises. I ask about them and he clams up, as if he's afraid to tell me about them."

"*Christ!* I should have seen this coming." Valentine played with a letter opener, smacking it against his palm. "There are COs here who'd still hate his guts if he pulled orphans out of a burning building. If he were in a coma they'd *still* think he was faking it."

The psychiatrist stood up and wandered to the window. "The literature on traumatic brain injury is fascinating, Case. In the nineteenth century there was a church-going law-abiding railroad worker in Vermont or New Hampshire, I forget which one. By all accounts, a very decent fellow. One day at work, he got an iron rod rammed through his frontal lobe. He didn't die, which is amazing enough in itself, but he turned into a lazy drunken violent slob who nobody could stand. Then there was a Dutch housepainter who fell off a ladder, landed on his head and woke up with psychic powers. He helped the police solve crimes they'd given up on. He had no idea how he did it, he just did. So now we have Ray Hazen, one of the three or four worst inmates I've ever seen, and he comes back here looking like he won't hurt a fly . . . you mark me, Case, they'll turn him into the same son of a bitch he was before."

Valentine threw himself back into his desk chair. "I've got to talk to Gunther. Don't know if it'll accomplish anything but I've got to try."

Valentine's meeting with Warden Gunther lasted less than five minutes. He began by voicing concerns about Ray's treatment. Not alone was it wrong, it was liable to have terrible consequences down the road. Gunther listened politely, thanked him for his interest and assured him that Mr. Hazen would be treated fairly. "Abusing him or any other inmate won't be tolerated," he stated flatly. Valentine reiterated his concern that this was exactly what was happening. Put simply, the COs were punishing Ray for a past he no longer had a connection with. Valentine understood their antipathy towards him. As a black man, he'd hardly been a fan himself . . . Gunther interrupted him and promised to look into it. Valentine launched into an account of personality changes following traumatic brain injury. "A fascinating subject," said Gunther, cutting him off again, "and I'd like to hear more about it, but I'm late for another meeting." Again, he thanked Valentine for his interest.

* * *

In mid-December the administration moved Ray back to A-Block. Case and Valentine wanted to keep him in the hospital wing. They figured it would be less likely for staff to abuse him there, but they found it hard to justify a longer stay. Ray's gait and balance were approaching normal. His pronunciation remained impaired but his vocabulary, grammar and syntax were close to what they'd been before the beating. Going strictly through channels, Ray had requisitioned magazines and a few books from the prison's library; he practiced reading and writing on his own.

On A-Block the COs kept Ray away from the blacks and Latinos as much as possible, per order of Warden Gunther. As Gunther told them off the record, he personally wouldn't mind it if Ray got himself beaten up again, or better yet killed, but the word would leak out. "The bleeding hearts would have a field day. Besides, the paperwork would be a nightmare."

They allowed him to have rec as long as he went out only with other whites. One day, one of them approached him. "Hey, ain't you Ray Hazen?"

Ray looked at him, trying not to show fear. "Uh huh." He'd learned that friendliness is rarely appropriate and much more apt to be dangerous. Besides, this new guy was someone you didn't want for an enemy. More than six feet tall, weighing twice as much as Ray did, with a *don't screw with me* look about him.

The new guy saw his fear. "Relax, dude. We was at Hickory Bluff together, we met in the Aryan Ramblers." Hickory Bluff was the state's largest juvenile facility, regarded as a finishing school for youthful sociopaths.

He offered a hand. "Name's Walker Calloway. You don't recognize me, huh?"

"There's lots I don't remember. They said I was in some kinda fight and got hit in the head."

"Yeah, I read about it. You made the news, my man. They almost killed you." He put a hand on Ray's shoulder. "Don't worry, ain't *no one* gonna pull that shit on you again, not when I'm around. We're family, see?"

"I'm glad you're here," said Ray. For the first time in weeks, he smiled.

*   *   *

Walker took Ray under his wing like a long-lost brother. In their brief times together, Walker told him of their common background in the Ramblers, throwing in a refresher course on white supremacy. He taught him exercises to do in his cell, pushups and squats and the like. *We gotta get you back in shape, see? You can't be no weak sister in this place.* Walker told him how to communicate by sending kites, illicit written messages, by way of the semi-trusted inmates who came around with food trays or the book cart. How to hit someone in a place that really hurt him, like his balls or throat. Ray absorbed these lessons avidly.

As Walker's tutelage progressed, Ray's eyes showed ever more of the old hostility. His pursed lips were often down-turned now. The changes weren't lost on Case and Valentine.

They met one afternoon in Valentine's office as Case summarized a meeting he'd had with Ray the day before. "I couldn't engage him. It was like pulling teeth. Whenever I brought something up, he didn't say much more than yes or no, or he ignored me altogether. I asked repeatedly what was wrong, but he just shook his head. After ten minutes, he asked to go back to his cell."

"That's eight more than he was willing to spend with me last week."

"He's taking up the old attitudes. I mentioned you yesterday, and he called you a . . ." Case blushed. "He used a racial slur. First time I heard him use one since he came back here." Valentine shut his eyes.

Meanwhile, Eduardo Lorca remained Ray's frequent visitor. As promised, he came into Ray's cell at random intervals, dumping his bedding and possessions in a heap as he searched for contraband, making him stand at attention, taunting him, slapping or punching him when he felt like it, threatening to put him in four-point restraints over bare bedsprings if he *looked* at him the wrong way. At first, Ray felt sick to his stomach when the Lieutenant headed toward him, but in time the sick feeling gave way to something else. A smoldering hate, not altogether unpleasant. In fact there was something heartening about it.

One day, when they met on the patio, Ray was quieter than usual. "What's the matter?" asked Walker.

"I gotta problem. With Lieutenant Lorca."

"I can't stand that worthless greaser," Calloway clucked sympathetically. "What's he done now, bro?"

"It's kinda hard to talk about."

"Tell me anyway."

At first, Ray wouldn't meet his eyes. "Well, I told you how he always tears my cell apart and looks for contraband. This time . . . this time he was lookin' for it in my, uh, body. He made me get undressed, and bend over and spread my cheeks. Then he put on a glove and felt around up there. He was rough, he really hurt me."

Walker, at first too angry to say anything, kicked the concrete patio with the heel of his boot; his flushed face looked almost purple. Then he put a hand on Ray's elbow. "Don't worry, we're gonna make him sorry he was ever born. Now here's my plan . . ." He spoke softly as they walked in slow ovals around the patio.

*   *   *

One of Orrington's times of relative laxity was sick call, which was always well attended. Escorted from cell blocks in small groups, inmates congregated in the hospital wing as they waited for a doctor, nurse or dentist. It gave them a chance to leave their cells, to seek treatment for ailments real or imagined. While waiting, they could talk among themselves, an uncommon opportunity. A number of COs waited with them. Lieutenant Lorca often served as the supervising officer.

One morning, Ray asked for a pass for sick call because of pain in his reconstructed knee. Walker asked for one too, claiming that he'd coughed up blood. They sat together, close to where Lorca stood scowling at them.

"What's wrong with you?" Walker asked Ray, loud enough to be overheard.

"My knee hurts."

"His knee hurts, poor baby," Walker said to no one in particular. "I swear, this guy's the biggest pussy we got here."

"Don't call me a pussy," warned Ray in as threatening a voice as he could muster.

Walker sneered. "What're you gonna do about it, girlfriend?"

"Lemme show you." Ray sprung to his feet and lunged at him, his arms flailing. The bigger man blocked his blows easily and grabbed Ray around the waist, bringing him to the ground with a thud.

"Code red!" yelled Lorca, the signal for a fight between inmates, before moving in to try to separate them. As he did, they turned on him, Ray pummeling his face and neck while Walker delivered sledgehammer blows to his midriff and kicked him repeatedly in the groin. By the time a flying squad of COs pulled them off, Lorca's face was a discolored mask of cuts and bruises; one of his eyes was swollen shut. His breathing was labored and shallow.

An inmate in almost any prison can do bodily harm to a CO, provided he's willing to pay the price for it. At Orrington, the price is very high. The COs beat Ray and Walker to the point of unconsciousness. When they finished, Gunther ordered four-point restraints over bedsprings for each of them. They would lose all privileges for three months, during which time they'd remain entirely in their cells. No visits, phone calls or commissary. They wouldn't be permitted to shower. Instead, they could clean themselves with water from the sink. COs yelled at them throughout the day and interrupted their sleep throughout the night; they put salt in their coffee and dead flies in their juice; sometimes they forgot to give them meals.

During Ray's second day in four-points, Case came into his cell, which now smelled powerfully of urine since Ray was rarely allowed up to relieve himself. Case sat on the stainless-steel toilet seat. "What happened?"

Spread-eagled on his stomach, Ray raised his head a few inches. "We got him good is what happened. He's been nasty to me ever since I got here, and we got him good." Ray tried to smile.

"How was he nasty?"

"He did all kinds of stuff." Ray recounted the routine dumping of his possessions, the slaps and punches, the ham-handed rectal examination.

"I wish you'd told us. Maybe we could have stopped it."

"Walker said it wouldn't matter. He said the COs do what they want and nothing changes." Ray tried to smile again. "I guess we made it change, at least for a moment."

"Yes, but look what happened to you. The truth is, Ray—and I don't like it any more than you do—they can pretty much do what they want to you. Besides, Lieutenant Lorca's sure to bring charges. That means you and Walker may get another ten or fifteen years added to your sentences. Maybe more."

"Whatever they do to us, it's worth it."

Case put a hand on Ray's sink to steady himself; the reek was making him lightheaded. He tried to think of something he might offer, words to break through Ray's rebuilt fortress. *Not everyone will treat you as Lieutenant Lorca did. Behave and you'll get out of here someday. If you become the way you were, you'll spend the rest of your life caught up in a circle of violence and retaliation, more violence and more retaliation. You proved it was possible for people to like you, and for you to like them in return. It doesn't have to be the way it was before.*

This advice struck Case as vacuous and unpersuasive. He wasn't sure he placed much stock in it himself.

*   *   *

One afternoon, Valentine got a phone call from Warden Gunther, asking him to come to his office right away. When he did, he saw that Gunther had another visitor, an officious young woman with small darting eyes. The warden introduced them. The woman was Ann Finch, an assistant state's attorney.

Gunther waved the doctor to a chair. "Ray Hazen will be transferred out of state," he said without preamble.

"Oh?"

"I'll let her tell the story." Gunther pointed towards the woman.

"I don't know if you remember this," Ms. Finch said, "but Ray has a sister."

Valentine nodded. "She left Vermont and no one heard from her again. No one knows if she's alive or dead."

"Oh, she's alive all right. She went out west . . . California, then Nevada. She used any drugs that she could find, became a prostitute, made pornographic films, got arrested five or six times. Her life was a train wreck. But during her last arrest, she cleaned up her act. She found religion, earned a GED, took college courses. After her release, she worked in a halfway house. She also went to church three times a week. At some point she became curious about her brother Ray. So she got on the Internet, and it didn't take her long to learn what happened. The arrests, the beating, everything."

"She ignores him for ten years, and suddenly she wants to be the good big sister. Warms your heart," muttered Gunther.

"In any case," Finch ignored him, "she began pushing for his transfer to Nevada. She figured the situation here was a stalemate, that Ray had made too many enemies for him to be treated fairly. Besides, she could visit him in Nevada. Have a positive effect on him, prepare him for reentering society."

"Do you believe it?" Gunther butted in again. "This born-again druggie hooker porn star comes from nowhere and wants to rehabilitate him!"

"There's more," resumed Finch. "If we *don't* agree to a transfer, she's threatening to sue us. She alleges that we violated his civil rights by not protecting him while he was in our custody. I'm sure she'd throw in punitive damages."

"If she did sue, would she have a shot?" asked Valentine.

"Maybe. She'd bring suit in federal court. Their chances would be better there." Finch paused. "The Attorney General is concerned about the negative publicity, as well as the possibility of losing a size-able sum of money. Juries don't usually much care for inmates, but Ray might prove an exception. He'd make a sympathetic witness, especially with the speech and gait impairment, and of course he'd play up his pain and suffering."

"Personally, I don't think it's such a bad idea for him to be transferred out of state," opined Valentine. "In view of what he and Calloway did to Lorca, his chances of getting out of here alive are close to nil. Let him go to a place where at least they aren't gunning for him. Besides, it's not as if we haven't done this kind of thing before."

Inmate swaps between states were fairly common, as they knew. States with especially overcrowded prisons negotiated with other states to take prisoners off their hands. An inmate might be deemed at risk in high-profile cases, or he might be part of a gang that needed to be broken up. Or, as with Ray Hazen, he might simply have made too many enemies in a given location.

"That's the Attorney General's stance," said Finch.

"Besides," continued the psychiatrist, "his sister might be useful to him. If she cleaned up her own act, maybe she could help him clean up his."

"Yeah, right," snapped Gunther. "And maybe he'll become a U.S. senator from Nevada." He picked up a letter opener from his desk and fiddled with it. "I suppose I can't complain," he said, less waspishly. "At least we'll get rid of him. Let him be Nevada's problem, let's see how *they* make out with him. I just wish we could keep him long enough to charge him with assaulting Eduardo—who's almost certain to have lasting disabilities, in case anyone's interested."

Valentine turned to Finch. "It's a done deal, then?" She nodded.

"When will he be going there?"

"The day after tomorrow."

*   *   *

Waiting with Ray on the day of his departure, in a small lounge next to the visiting room, Case studied him. The reconstructive surgeons had done fine work, and you had to look carefully to see the facial scars. Unless he smiled or talked, you hardly noticed the missing teeth. He now looked too old to be a college boy but, except for the orange prison jumpsuit, handcuffs and ankle cuffs, he might have passed for a bookstore clerk or bank teller.

"So, Ray, another hour and you'll be out of here."

"That's right," said Ray, his tone flat.

"I guess you won't miss it much."

"I'll miss Walker. Only friend I had here. If it weren't for him, I'd still be takin' crap from Lieutenant Lorca. Walker took my side, even when he knew they'd beat him up the same as me." Case couldn't disagree. Whatever he might think of Walker Calloway, the man had put himself on the line for someone else.

He changed the subject. "How long since you've seen your sister?"

"Fifteen years or so." Ray's loss of visiting privileges had precluded a recent meeting. "Doesn't matter, since I don't hardly remember her anyway."

"Maybe you'll remember more about her when you have a chance to spend some time together."

"Maybe." Case couldn't tell if Ray was prepared to like her or regard her as someone to be won over, used and duped.

They fell silent. The social worker felt compelled to send him off with a modicum of encouragement. "You can make a fresh start there," he said finally. "The people in Nevada will be new to you and you to them. Some of them might treat you decently if you give them half a chance."

"How do I know they won't be like Lieutenant Lorca?"

"You don't. Maybe they will and maybe not. But you could meet them with an open mind and wait and see."

Ray looked skeptical. "What if there's lots of spics and niggers there? Walker, he says they're the worst ones, and you gotta defend yourself against 'em. He says we're better than they are, and whites got no business with 'em."

"Ray, you need to decide for yourself about the ones you'll meet. I know Walker's your friend, but that doesn't make everything he says the truth. And I suggest you not call people names like that. They're ugly words, they'll get you in a world of trouble. Besides, do you remember where you were before you came to Orrington?"

"Yeah, that hospital where they taught me to walk and do things again. What about it?"

"Well, you said black people tried to help you there. You liked them. Remember how much you wanted to go back?" Ray made no answer.

Case tried another tack. "There'll be more for you to do out there, compared to here."

"But I'll still be in prison."

"Yes, but it won't be as restrictive as this place." Ray's sister's lawyer had managed to have him sent to a medium-security facility. "You may be able to go to classes. Work on your reading and writing, for example. Get some training so you can find a job when you get out."

Ray turned and looked him in the eye. "You really think they'll let me out someday?"

Case paused. "I think so, provided that you don't make trouble. That you don't get into fights or give the COs a hard time."

"I can't remember being on the outside. Can't

imagine what it's like."

The social worker chose his words carefully. "Well, it'll take some getting used to. You'll have the freedom to make decisions for yourself. Sometimes they'll be good ones, sometimes not. You'll have the freedom to do things that'll hurt you, like hanging out with the wrong people. If you do, chances are that you'll get yourself locked up again. You'll be right back where you started."

"How do I know if a decision is the right one?"

"You think it through. *If I do this, then so and so will happen; but if I do that, then such and such will happen.* You also ask people you trust, who care about you. Your sister, for one."

"I don't know her, not really, so how'm I supposed to trust her?"

Case began to frame an answer when a key turned in the door to the lounge. Warden Gunther entered, a CO on each side, another one behind him. He nodded curtly in Case's direction without quite looking at him. Then he glanced at Ray with obvious distaste.

"Time to leave, Hazen," he said between clenched teeth. "There's a van outside that'll take you directly to the airport."

Case glanced at Ray. His eyes, irate and defiant, reminded Case of the Ray of old. *Do your worst. You will not break me.* But there was something else in them, something less antagonistic, hinting of a receptivity to kindness. Something that brought to mind the man-child who'd returned to Orrington, who didn't see everyone as an enemy until proven otherwise. Who might appreciate a slab of homemade sweet potato pie without throwing it back in the face of the giver.

Case shook his hand and wished him well. Surrounded by his escorts, Ray walked in small, awkward steps—the ankle cuffs allowed him to move no more than inches at a time—and headed to the waiting van.

HATER

I. THANKSGIVING DINNER WITH UNCLE BUTCH

In the course of his fifteen incarcerations, Walker Calloway had met with at least that many shrinks. He lumped them into three main groups: rookies just completing residencies and needing the money, or semi-retired burnouts, or gooks and curry-heads who barely spoke English. Most of them he held in low regard. Unbelievable, the naïveté of some of them. If he told them his first sexual encounter had been with a kangaroo, they might have believed him.

He'd found a few he liked, though. Among these was Herbert Valentine. An odd couple, Walker and Dr. Valentine—Walker, a career racist, and Valentine, an African-American. But the doctor's candor and nonjudgmental manner prompted Walker to put aside his bias. He engaged in a kind of doublethink: *Blacks are subhuman, inferior to whites in every way, but this one's pretty decent, smart enough and okay to talk to.* Valentine ran Mental Health Services at Orrington, a maximum-security prison.

One day, as they sat drinking coffee, discussion focused on Walker's mother lode of rage. "When do you first remember being angry?" asked Valentine.

"Can't hardly recall when I wasn't. But it might have been the Thanksgiving just after I turned four. Thanksgiving dinner with Ma and Uncle Butch. Good ole Butch . . ." Walker looked about to spit.

"Butch wasn't no real uncle to me. Ma liked me to call her boyfriends uncles, don't know why. Anyway, she and Butch lived together a coupla years after Pa died." Artie Calloway, Walker's father, had fallen asleep on a railroad track after unwinding with Four Roses and several joints.

"Butch was as useless a piece of shit as ever lived," continued Walker. "Scarecrow-thin, thick ugly black eyebrows. Always scowled, like he just smelled the world's worst fart. One minute he'd treat you okay, next minute he'd turn on you, quick as a rattlesnake. My birthday's November nineteenth and he'd actually been pretty good to me. Gave me a tricycle, which he probably stole."

"So, a week later and it was Thanksgiving—"

"Yeah. And Butch was in a mood. We knew as soon as he came down for breakfast, looking like he wanted to kick a dog."

Walker sipped coffee. "All day we waited for the explosion . . . Ma, my sister Bernadette and me. Ma kept leaning over backwards in that pathetic way of hers, *Butch, honey, how about another beer?* By dinnertime he was hammered. Now Ma was pretty much a bungler, but she was always a right fine cook, especially at Thanksgiving. Roast turkey, candied yams, apple pie made from scratch, the works. She and Bernadette and me set the table while Butch sat on his ass in the living room, on his sixth or his tenth beer or whatever. Then we sat down to eat."

"What happened?"

"She asked him to give a blessing. Bad move. Don't know why it riled him, but with Butch there didn't have to be no reason. He started to rant about how there wasn't a goddamn thing to be thankful for, what with these miserable people around him who didn't care if he worked himself to death so they could live comfortably—which was a crock since mostly he was too drunk to work, got fired every other month. How he'd hooked up with a stupid cow who didn't do squat except tend to her brats. He stood up . . . with one hand he threw the turkey on the floor, with the other he flung the yams against the wall. And then he stormed off."

"That's when you first remember hating him?"

"Yeah. I'm sure I did before, but that's the first time I was aware of it. Before, what I felt was fear. This was different, though. Hate overcame the fear. He was big and I was small, but it didn't matter. Hate was the equalizer."

II. FATHER FLYNN

After Butch came Uncle Ralph, who never brushed his greenish teeth, and Uncle Boyd, who gave Walker's mother a black eye because she made his coffee too weak, and too many others to keep track of. Some of them lasted a year or so, others left in weeks. Walker despised them all.

Life at school was no better than at home. Antsy and distracted, Walker made terrible grades; his teachers regarded him as unteachable. Classmates avoided him as much as possible.

One place where he found something like tranquility was in their church, St. Brendan's. He liked the music, the smell of incense, the glow of the votive candles, the otherworldliness. He liked the quiet and safety there, with no fake uncles to beat him, no teachers in his face. He especially liked Father Flynn.

Benedict Flynn's height, six foot two, and his thick white hair gave him the look of a family doctor in a soap opera. He had wide-set blue eyes and a full-lipped mouth. Handsome, notwithstanding his slightly hooked nose and the scars from his teenage acne. In his late forties, fit and trim, he could have passed for thirty-five if his hair hadn't whitened early.

Father Flynn took a special interest in the parish children. His parishioners' lives were rife with poverty, violence, drugs and alcohol—and the children bore the brunt of all of it. He played basketball and threw horseshoes with them, arranged outings to a children's museum and an aquarium. He went camping with them, paying for most of the food and equipment out of pocket. Whenever possible, he met with them one to one, inviting them to his study with its overstuffed chairs and walnut paneling.

Walker became one of Father Flynn's special boys, coming to his study for conversation, moral support and informal counseling, accompanied by milk and the housekeeper's homemade treats. They talked about Jesus, but more often about Walker's mother and the uncles, and what he wanted to do when he finished school. And they talked of lighter matters. The Yankees, and *Beavis and Butt-head*, and who made better hamburgers, McDonald's or Wendy's.

Later, Walker tried to remember when the other things had started. It might have been one day when he began to cry, a rare occurrence for him, and Father Flynn put an arm around his shoulder and stroked his neck. Or when Walker told him that his Aunt Dee, his favorite relative, had kidney cancer. Father Flynn patted his knee, and his hand stayed too long on Walker's leg. The touching made Walker jumpy, but there was something comforting about it too. Something welcome, even. The truth was, he craved male company. Walker dimly remembered Artie Calloway as a nonentity, always dazed by booze and marijuana. The uncles' version of intimacy had been to hit him. Father Flynn's attention was altogether different, even longed-for.

One day, a bit after Walker's twelfth birthday, an early blizzard caused school closures. He made an unplanned visit to St. Brendan's, and Father Flynn brought him to the study. As they ate date bars and drank hot chocolate, conversation turned to sex.

"You're becoming a man," the priest noted. "You're two inches taller than last summer. Your voice is deeper too."

"I guess," Walker mumbled. He didn't like to talk about this stuff.

"You'll be going through all sorts of changes. Your life will be completely different."

"Uh huh."

What happened next was like a poorly made home movie, indistinct and choppy. Father Flynn told him that he needn't be ashamed of himself and his new man's body and its urges, the Church was now less strict about such matters, and men—the group included Walker now—should feel comfortable expressing fondness for each other, there was no harm in a touch or hug or even a kiss. Jesus understood the power of these feelings. Jesus, always there for us, even in the darkest times, understood more about us than we understood about ourselves. As with everything, Jesus remained infinitely accepting and forgiving.

Father Flynn locked the door, and Walker found himself lying naked on the floor. Stroking him, the priest gently but firmly turned him over. The boy was on his stomach now, not moving, afraid to move, more afraid than he'd ever been. Walker felt the priest's weight on his back, felt the priest's breath against the side of his neck. *It's all right, son . . . It's all right . . .*

That's all he let himself remember.

Walker couldn't say how often it happened. Five times, or ten or fifteen? It didn't matter. What mattered was that it had happened once.

III. HICKORY BLUFF

Walker sulked his way through early adolescence, attending school when he felt like it, which he usually didn't. He hung around with a like-minded cluster of youths who drank, smoked pot and ripped off smaller kids for lunch money. He shoplifted and broke into cars. A favorite pastime: bashing mailboxes with baseball bats. His mother, preoccupied with a new boyfriend, Uncle Julio, ignored him. Despite a blank smile resulting from his fifty LSD trips, and an inability to complete a sentence of more than six words, Julio was a cut above the other uncles. He made steady money at a carwash; he wasn't violent.

*   *   *

At fifteen, Walker hit a teacher with an uppercut that broke his jaw. They sent him to Hickory Bluff, a facility for juvenile offenders.

Hickory Bluff was a pleasant-looking cluster of red brick dorms, a school building that doubled as a dining hall, an administrative center, and a white chapel complete with spire. Situated on a gently rolling countryside along a riverbank, its pathways crisscrossed well-trimmed lawns. The residents, boys from twelve to eighteen, wore street clothes instead of prison khakis. Except for barbed wire and the guardhouse, you might take it for the campus of a small attractive college.

Hickory Bluff was Walker's home for the better part of four years.

IV. THE ARYAN RAMBLERS

The Department of Corrections officially ran Hickory Bluff, but in fact it was run by gangs. To join a gang was a near-necessity. While it didn't turn your life into a cakewalk, it did keep you from being routinely beaten, robbed and sodomized.

Shortly after his arrival, Walker joined a white power group, the Aryan Ramblers. Its members became his friends and brothers, his mentors and protectors. They taught him such skills as making a lethal weapon from a toothbrush and defending himself with a blow to an opponent's throat, groin or shin. They taught him about the white man's superiority over lesser types, particularly blacks, Jews and Latinos. They passed around *Mein Kampf* to Walker and the other probationers, quizzing them on its contents as if it were the

Baltimore Catechism. Question: *What is the purpose of propaganda?* Answer: *To emphasize what one sets out to argue for, and convince the masses.* Question: *How did Hitler define democracy?* Answer: *"The deceitful theory that all men are created equal."* They taught him the importance of blind loyalty and they honed his aptitude for hating, already considerable.

Only one person, Mr. Banks, tried to counteract their influence. Lyman Banks, affable and low-key, taught history and English. His receding hairline and heavy-lidded eyes made him look older than his forty years.

Walker went to classes regularly. Skipping them meant he'd lose TV or commissary privileges, but he would have attended anyway. They broke up the crushing boredom of life at Hickory Bluff. Besides, the Ramblers had fueled a tiny flame of curiosity in him. He especially wanted to know more of history. Who was this Hitler anyway? Who were these Jews he despised so much? (Walker himself had never met one.) And—he knew enough not to ask the other Ramblers about this—if Hitler had been such a genius, why did he lose the war?

Mr. Banks, taking note of Walker's curiosity, offered to meet with him individually after class. Walker agreed to do so, albeit with misgivings after Father Flynn. But now he was six feet tall and weighed 195; he'd beat Banks senseless if the teacher tried anything funny.

*   *   *

"When you study history, you learn different ways of interpreting what happened," Mr. Banks explained.

"What's that supposed to mean?" asked Walker, not one for subtlety.

"Take World War II. Contrary to what the Ramblers tell you, most people are glad that Germany lost—"

"That's only 'cause of Jew propaganda," Walker interrupted. "Like that bullshit about concentration camps."

"You don't think they existed?"

"'Course not," Walker scoffed.

"You can visit them, you know. Auschwitz and several others. You can see for yourself. Plus, there's the testimony of witnesses—"

"Jews got all the money in the world," Walker interrupted him again. "They *buy* witnesses."

Banks tried another tack. "After the war, Eisenhower went to one of the camps himself. He saw the ovens and gas chambers, the pits full of bodies. He said he wanted to bear witness—Ike himself, the Allied

Supreme Commander, the future president. If people ever doubted what had happened, he said they had his testimony."

"He coulda lied. Or the Jews coulda gotten to him too. Bought him out." Walker felt uneasy, though. A great uncle, long dead, had fought in World War II and lost an arm at Normandy. The family regarded him as a hero.

Banks knew better than to attack the Ramblers directly; they gave too much to Walker. All the teacher could do was to reach out to him and to leave him open to the possibility that the Ramblers had it wrong. At times, the boy responded to these overtures. He spoke about his mother and the uncles. He told Banks what had happened to his father, something he'd shared only with Father Flynn. He told him that he hoped to marry and have children of his own one day, although the prospect terrified him. *What if he botched the job the way his parents had?*

Two high-ranking Ramblers, Al Payson and Hughie Lansing, approached Walker in the dorm one evening. They were nice about it, but they said he spent too much time with Mr. Banks. "Besides," Al told him, "we got it on good authority that Banks is Jewish."

Walker never met alone with him again. He clammed up in class, even when he wanted to ask a question or make a comment. In the end, Banks gave up on him, the way his other teachers had. The Ramblers' influence was unopposed.

V. ORRINGTON

When Walker left Hickory Bluff, two weeks before his eighteenth birthday, he had no high school diploma and no family support—his mother had moved 2,000 miles away, to Houston with Uncle Julio. Fully grown at six foot two and 220, Walker wore his chestnut hair in a greasy ponytail. He could distill alcoholic beverages from fruit and sugar, kill a man with his bare hands and quote paragraphs of *Mein Kampf* by heart, but he couldn't drive a truck or operate a cash register; his marketable skills were close to nil. He worked as a flagman for the Highway Department, a kitchen helper at a hospital and an assistant custodian at a movie complex, but his money came mainly from small-time drug deals and petty theft.

Living in a miniscule apartment above a Kinko's, he spent much of his time watching TV, usually cartoons and cop show reruns, although he did see a few programs on the History Channel. But he kept fit despite his indolence, pumping iron and using the stationary bike at a no-frills health club.

Although he'd hated his father's alcoholism, he began to drink heavily himself. A six-pack or two became routine. He didn't share Artie's taste for pot (it made him goofy, it softened his fighting edge), but now and again he liked cocaine. He favored drinking at the titty bars, where his big indulgence was a lap dance.

Arrested often, he served shorter bids, weeks or months, at the county jail. As his offenses grew more serious—assaults and stickups instead of larcenies, conspiracy to sell instead of possession—he began serving time in prison. His sentences lengthened.

In prison, he established a reputation as a hard-ass. They routinely found contraband in his cell, mainly improvised weapons. He frequently got into fights, especially with blacks and Latinos. He got a lot of tickets—disciplinary write-ups—and spent long stretches in punitive isolation.

One day, at a medium-security prison, a black CO named Rollie Sims heard him proclaim that Jesus would be a racist nowadays. Walker was prepared for Sims's anger, but the CO roared with laughter. "Calloway," he said when he stopped, "you're so full of shit it's amazing you can stand upright."

Some things are simply unacceptable, like being ridiculed by a black man. Walker landed a blow to

Sims's midriff, felling him like a shot bird. They transferred Walker to Orrington, a facility housing the state's most violent and intransigent inmates.

Shortly after he arrived at Orrington, Walker encountered another Aryan Rambler, Ray Hazen, a fellow Hickory Bluff alumnus who'd acquired a number of enemies. They included a CO named Eduardo Lorca; Ray had thrown a mixture of urine and feces at him. Lieutenant Lorca didn't have a forgiving nature, and he devoted himself to making Ray's life as miserable as possible. When Ray confided in Walker, they devised a plan to attack Lorca as they waited one day for sick call. They landed a flurry of blows and kicks to his face, guts and groin before the unconscious CO was dragged to safety.

VI. IRIS

After the assault on Lieutenant Lorca, Walker spent three months in seg. The COs beat Ray and him almost as badly as the two of them had beaten Lorca. The COs kept up a barrage of harassments—spitting in Walker's coffee, shining lights in his eyes throughout the night, whatever else occurred to them. The only time he left his cell for more than a few hours a week was when he went to court to face a new assault charge. Copping a plea, he got ten years suspended after eight, to be served upon completion of his original sentence.

When they finally returned him to general population, Walker was different. Fractionally more subdued. He no longer went out of his way to antagonize blacks and Latinos. In addition to his contraband copy of *Mein Kampf*, he read a hodgepodge of other things: the Bible, yellowed James Bond paperbacks, in-flight magazines left on the book cart by COs back from vacations. *The Executioner's Song* by Norman Mailer, which he liked until someone told him that Mailer was a Jew. He started attending Mass again, even though he regarded priests as hypocrites and scumbags.

He'd also begun a correspondence with a woman, Iris.

One day, a CO delivered a blue envelope addressed to him in an unfamiliar hand.

Dear Walker, the letter read, *My name is Iris Warren. We never met and you're probably wondering who I am and why I'm writing. Well, my pastor, Rev. Irby, started a program where we write to people in prison. It's not a religious program. Rev. Irby thought it might be nice if you had more contact with the outside world, which he figured is pretty limited.*

I never wrote a letter like this before and I don't

know where to begin. Well, I guess I should tell you about myself. For starters I'm 35. I had a few long relationships but never married. Guess I was kind of wild in my teens and early 20s, did things I'm not proud of, but my life is finally going in a good direction. I work as a waitress at an Olive Garden. When I'm not working I spend most of my time with my sister and her kids. I also like bowling and hiking. Church wasn't much to me when I was growing up but it's an important part of my life now.

If you'd like to write to me and I hope you do, I'd like to know about you too. I'm interested in what life's like in prison if you care to share that with me. Pretty frightening, I guess. Hope your spirits are holding up. God bless you. Sincerely, Iris

He wrote her back the same day.

Dear Iris, he began, *It was a real nice surprise to hear from you. I don't get much mail mainly a postcard from my mother or my sister both out West. Your right my contact with the outside is limited. Haven't had visitors for 2 years except for lawyers.*

Not used to writing about myself neither but here goes. I'm 34. Been here 7 years. Shoulda been released by now but a friend & me got into a beef with a guard and that added time. Sometimes wonder if I'll live long enough to get out & sometimes I don't care. Must sound strange but it's true. The outside don't appeal to me like you might think. Here at least you know what to expect from people, not much.

No family to speak of, at least close by. Always been a loner except for these guys I hang with. We call ourselves The Aryan Ramblers. I know you hear bad things about gangs but we're loyal to each other & we protect each other & that means a lot to me.

You asked about life here. Main thing is everything's scheduled, not just meals and visits but showers & rec too & when you go to the law library or commissary. Another thing, nothing is private, people checking on you even when you sleep & wash & use the bathroom. But you get used to it. You turn inward.

Also I spend more time reading than before. Including the Bible. Went to church regular as a kid but things happened & I let it slide but I'm getting back to it. Been carrying a lot of anger for as long as I can remember & I know that's no good. Maybe reading the Bible & going to Mass will help me get rid of it.

That's about it for now. Thanks for the letter & hoping you keep writing.

Your friend, Walker

They wrote each other every week, sometimes more. She told him about the woman eating at the restaurant who had a laughing jag and sprayed Chianti and fettuccine across the table, and he told her about the crazy bastard who spent two years at a funny farm, who heard termites chewing on his brain. He wrote about his mother and the uncles, and she wrote about her mother taking off when she was six. He wrote about Hickory Bluff, and she wrote about her high school days, coming to an algebra exam too stoned to sign her name on the paper.

Her letters became the high points of his life.

She sent him a small blurred picture that showed a woman of uncertain age, a woman who could have been twenty-five or forty, with a round face and dark curly hair; impossible to tell the color of her eyes. A dark brown sweater concealed her figure.

He asked her to visit. Yes, she wrote back, she'd wanted to for months. She'd just about given up hope that he would ask.

VII. YOUR BASIC AMERICAN DREAM

Walker paced as he waited for her, his face scrubbed, his long hair shampooed and neat.

She arrived at precisely 2:15, when visiting hours started. He quickly took in details of her appearance.

She was a large woman, almost as tall as he was, not fat but solid. A pretty mouth, reddish tan lipstick. Slightly pug nose. Her skin showed a smoker's early mottling. Lively green eyes were her best feature. His verdict: altogether presentable.

Despite their increasingly intimate letters, they were shy when they came face to face. On opposite sides of a glass partition, they communicated by red phones. "Well now," he broke the silence, "it's real nice meeting you, at last."

Iris half-smiled at him. "Same here."

"Must be funny for you being in a place like this."

She shrugged. "It's not the first time I set foot inside a prison."

"Oh, yeah?"

"I was nineteen or twenty, in my wild phase. My boyfriend got arrested. First time I visited, I thought I'd have a heart attack. But I got used to it."

"People get used to just about anything."

"So I've noticed."

With that, they talked nonstop. Their conversation, like their letters, ranged widely, from the Bible to Olive Garden doings to the Yankees. By tacit agreement they avoided problematic areas like Walker's violent history and his involvement with the Ramblers. The visit passed in a flash.

"I hope you come again," he said as it concluded.

"You know I will."

"And keep writing. Your letters mean the world to me."

*　　*　　*

Walker made a sustained effort to stay out of trouble. Doing as he was told, he didn't mouth off to the COs, even when they tried hard to provoke him. He kept his cell spotless and free of contraband. His racist views remained unchanged, but he no longer trumpeted them.

After passing the GED, his high school equivalency exam, he took computer classes, using Orrington's small collection of antique IBMs and Dells. He also learned the rudiments of carpentry and plumbing. The warden had rejected his first two applications for the classes since they involved tools that could be used as weapons. But a pattern of Walker's improved behavior allowed him to overcome his qualms, and he approved the third one.

Iris visited as often as she could.

Dear Iris, he wrote, *It's always hard for me to ask for things. People let me down me when I do. But I gotta take a chance & ask something of you. Please wait for me. I'm sure there are men who come on to you better men than me & why wouldn't they. & I'm sure you get lonely & have a woman's needs.*

My rap sheet goes back to my teens, been locked up more than I been out. When I came here I was filled with hate, less now but there's still too much. You may wonder what a man like me can offer you. All I can say, I'll try my best to make a go of it when I'm released. To be better than I was. & I'll always love you & be grateful that your in my life.

What I want isn't so special. A job & home & enough $ to be comfortable. Sure I wouldn't mind being rich but comfortable is fine. But more than anything I wanna be with the woman I'm crazy about namely you.

Guess you could call it your basic American dream. Love, Walker

Despite Lorca's objections ("That piece of shit will be back here in a year!" predicted the enraged Lieutenant), they released Walker six years after he and Ray attacked him. Since Iris, Walker had turned into a model prisoner.

VIII. REENTRY

Walker left Orrington at thirty-nine, as happy as he'd ever been despite some uneasiness about how he'd deal with the freedom and lack of structure. Still, the future had never looked so bright to him. He'd be able to take a shower or a walk without anyone's permission. He could buy cigarettes at a 7-Eleven at 2AM if he felt like it. He might even find a decent job, thanks to his classes. He wouldn't go back to robbery or dealing.

He held to his racist views but resigned himself to living in a society where blacks, Jews and Latinos could gain power and prominence. "No one said I gotta like 'em," he told Iris during one of her visits, "just tolerate 'em."

The main thing: Iris would be there for him. Iris, with her green eyes that took him in with a warmth and acceptance he'd never known before, and her body promising comfort and safety. Iris, whom he'd never touched, whom he knew only as a letter writer and a figure on the other side of a glass partition.

They released him on a mid-May afternoon, the sun near-blinding in its brightness. In the parking lot they finally held each other, their embrace eager but tentative. Despite the day's warmth he felt her shiver.

At first they said little as she drove to her apartment in her ageing Subaru, washed and vacuumed in his honor. But gradually they fell into their usual give and take. They talked about the weather, and the Yankees' chances in the new baseball season, and she asked what kind of restaurant he'd prefer on this, his first day out of prison. He said it didn't matter as long as he could get a steak and onion rings.

Conversation swerved to the more personal. He told her of his last days in prison—his resolve to keep his cool, no matter what anyone said or did; he'd give them no excuse for not releasing him. She told him the girls at work had chipped in to buy her a gift certificate for Victoria's Secret, to get herself something special for his arrival.

"Pull over."

When she did, he kissed her, cupping her face in his hands like a chalice.

*   *   *

No easy thing, their living together. On his part, he'd lived only with other men, in cell or dormitory, for over twenty years. He'd learned a basic rule of prison: to avoid displays of friendliness or courtesy lest they be seen as weakness, a first step towards becoming someone's pussy. Sleep, of necessity, became light and uneasy, lest one be awoken by a punch or kick, or worse. He tossed and turned, waking up whenever Iris shifted in the bed. Once, when she reached out and touched his arm, he almost hit her.

On her part, Iris had lived alone since a former fiancé had shoved her against a wall and walked out on her six years earlier. Neat and orderly, she had to accustom herself to a man who left whiskers and blobs of shaving cream in the sink, who drank milk straight from the carton and who rarely emptied an ashtray. Iris herself had quit smoking.

It took him two months to find a job. People were cordial until they read his application and came to the part about felony convictions. "I know I made mistakes," he told them, looking them in the eye, "but I did the time, and all I'm looking for is a chance to make a fresh start." They promised to get back to him but never did.

She tried to help him. Someone she knew owned a cleaning service, and they could always use an extra man. A friend's husband did landscaping. Walker accepted part-time jobs from them; they paid little and included no benefits.

There were good moments. When she got home from work, they sat on the couch and had a beer as they counted up her tips. They joked about how they'd spend the money. "Think we should buy a Corvette or a Jaguar?" he wondered out loud on a particularly good night, when she brought home more than $200. Then they undressed and retired to her king-sized bed. He never ceased to marvel that a loving woman lay beside him, someone with whom he hadn't traded sex for drugs, someone who was there by choice.

The cleaning service lost several accounts that winter, and the landscaping work died altogether. Walker spent increasing time alone in their apartment. Bored and at loose ends, he drank. A beer or two became a six-pack; a glass of wine became an entire bottle. The beer and wine gave way to Yukon Jack and schnapps. His mood darkened as he drank more.

"I'm worried about you, sugar," Iris told him.

"Yeah? How come?"

"Because you don't care about anything. You always seem so angry. You hardly ever smile anymore . . ." She put a hand on his elbow. He pulled his arm away.

"There ain't much to smile about."

"Well, I don't know. There's food on the table, a roof over our heads. Plus, we have each other."

"Uh huh." He swigged Yukon Jack.

"Listen, sugar, I know they've been a rough few months. But it'll get better soon, I know it will."

"Why should it? Things won't get better till white men get the balls to reclaim the country, and I don't see that happening just now."

Knowing better than to argue when he did his Great White Number, as she called it, she changed the subject. "You should start coming to church with me again." They'd gone together throughout the spring and summer, but his attendance had dwindled. For three months, he hadn't gone at all.

"That's for saps. Might as well believe in the goddamn tooth fairy. I got better things to do on Sunday mornings."

It was difficult to make Iris angry but not impossible. "I'd appreciate it," she said icily, "if you not attack my religion. And I don't see what you do on Sunday mornings that's so important. Sleeping till noon because you've got another hangover. Reading those ridiculous pamphlets about how you're superior to everyone . . ."

His fist hit the kitchen table, hard enough to send his ashtray and the Yukon Jack flying. "You don't know *shit!*"

Blood drained from Iris's face. Her hands trembled but her voice stayed even. "I'm not a genius—"

"Ain't that the truth!"

"I'm not a genius," she tried again, "but I know some things. I know when someone's wasting his life by drinking too much and feeling sorry for himself. I know when he blames others for what's wrong with him—"

"Watch it, bitch. I'm warning you." Walker rarely yelled; his voice got quieter as he got angrier. Now it was a muted rumble.

But Iris was disinclined to watch it. "Those letters from prison . . . you used to write about your father. How he drank and did drugs and squandered opportunities. I hate to say this, Walker, but I wonder if you're following in his footsteps."

There it was: the last straw, a comparison with the late Artie Calloway. A man who stumbled through his bad joke of a life, his brain ravaged by marijuana and cheap booze, who never worked more than a month or two at a stretch and never earned more than minimum wage. A man so amazingly stupid that he lacked the sense not to fall asleep on railroad tracks.

Walker reached across the table and hit her full-force across the mouth. She gasped as her head jerked to the side. Despite his wrath, regret came in an instant. *Christ, what have I done?*

Iris rubbed her mouth, saying nothing, barely breathing. "I'll put a few things together and spend the night at my sister's," she said finally. "When I come back tomorrow, I want you gone. Take what you like, just go."

"Iris, I don't know what got into me." Still sitting, he felt his legs weaken; he would have toppled over if he'd tried to stand. "It won't happen again, I swear it."

"You're right, it won't." She looked at him dispassionately. "I think you're basically a decent man. In spite of yourself, I might add. But I've been in too many bad relationships, and I won't stay in another one. Not for you, not for anyone. I just won't."

She stood up, went to the bedroom and got an overnight case from the closet. Fifteen minutes later, she was out the door.

IX. RUNNING ON EMPTY

"What happened after you split up?" asked Valentine, several years after the fact.

Walker played with a rubber band from the doctor's desk. "I ran on empty," he said listlessly. "Found another place, a real dump. Stayed home and watched TV, cartoons and crap like that, same as when I left Hickory Bluff."

He contemplated the rubber band as if it held a secret meaning. "I lived on junk food—potato chips, donuts, Froot Loops right outta the box. Maybe I'd make a ham sandwich if I felt ambitious. Gained thirty pounds. I worked when I had to, a few days here, a few days there. Landscaping, cleaning toilets at the airport, jobs like that. Mostly, I drank."

"How much?"

"As much as I could get. A six-pack and a pint of Captain Morgan was typical. Knew I'd die if I kept it up, which is maybe what I wanted. The old man woulda been proud of me. I followed in his footsteps, like Iris said."

"Were there any other people in your life? Relatives or friends?"

"Not hardly. Ma was still in Houston. Bernadette was out in Oregon, on her fourteenth marriage or whatnot." He paused. "Well, I did have one friend, sort of. Kevin."

X. THE EMERALD LOUNGE

Nine months after Iris kicked him out, Kevin Zorn dropped by Walker's apartment one night. They'd done landscaping together, and sometimes they went out drinking. They also shared whatever drugs they got their hands on. Kevin, taller than Walker but less solidly built, had a mat of reddish-brown hair and dully malevolent dark eyes.

He arrived close to eight. Walker sat in his living room in jeans and a sleeveless undershirt, smoking a cigarette while he swigged vodka straight from the bottle.

"What's up?" Kevin asked.

"The usual. Nothing."

Kevin scanned the living room, surveying pizza boxes and cartons of Chinese takeout, beer and vodka bottles, newspapers and articles of clothing. "Ever think about cleaning up this place?"

"If you don't like it, feel free to get the fuck out."

"I'm just saying—"

"You're just saying *what?*" asked Walker, his voice a rasp.

Kevin respected Walker's temper. "Forget about it. Let's take off, get a few drinks somewhere. I'll buy, I got paid Friday."

Walker nodded, his anger assuaged by the prospect of free booze. "We could go to that place on Sycamore, the Emerald Lounge."

"Sure, why not?"

Walker belched, took the most presentable of his sweatshirts from the floor and put it on.

The Emerald Lounge consisted of an L-shaped

bar surrounded by candlelit booths and tables. Its dark green walls were bare except for incongruous travel posters—Ireland, Hawaii, Barbados. Walker and Kevin glanced at their fellow patrons: two couples in booths, a party of men in biker threads at one of the bigger tables, a pair of fiftyish women who drank beer and ate pretzels.

Walker and Kevin took seats at the bar, alternating Buds and shots of Canadian. At the end of the bar a man sat alone; they hadn't noticed him at first. About forty-five, his graying hair impeccably trimmed, he wore charcoal slacks, a blue sport coat and a burgundy shirt open at the collar. The only patron who drank wine.

"Take a look at Fancy Pants," said Kevin. "What's *he* doing here?"

"I dunno. Slumming, wants to see how the other half lives." Walker glanced towards him, his eyes glowing with contempt. "Just look at him. Most guys, they put on clothes and that's that. This guy looks like he primped like a goddamn girl. Ten to one he's a faggot. *God*, I hate fags!"

The man could see them talking but was too far away to hear them. He looked in their direction, smiling. Walker ignored him; Kevin nodded back.

When they finished the round, the bartender

brought over a beer and shot for each of them. "Compliments of the gentleman"—he pointed to the man in the blue sport coat.

"Isn't that something?" muttered Kevin, bemused.

"Uh huh."

"Poor bastard's probably lonely. Least we could do is ask him over."

Walker said nothing as he studied the top of the bar, where damp patches remained from their glasses. Then he turned to Kevin, a tight grim smile on his face. "Yeah, maybe we should."

The man, Cory Rose, chatted readily about his life. His company had transferred him from San Francisco. At first the move upset him. He had friends in California; he'd lived there ever since his college graduation. When his boss told him about the transfer, he thought about quitting. "Thing is," explained Cory, his speech slightly slurred, "the company always paid me well and treated me fairly. I thought I'd wait and see how it'd be here." The move had been less than three months ago, and he still didn't know how he felt about the city. "Okay, I guess, but not the easiest place to meet folks. San Francisco's much friendlier. Besides, I'll miss the 49ers' games." He'd had season tickets.

Cory tried to engage his companions. What kind of work did they do? Were they from here? Did they like the city? Were they members of a health club? He hadn't had the chance to join one but he planned to, and he was open to suggestions. Frequently on the road, he found it hard to keep in shape. Were they married? He asked this last question with studied casualness.

Cory drank more wine and bought Walker and Kevin another round; his speech became more slurred. Walker said he needed to use the bathroom. Catching Kevin's eye, he indicated for him to come too.

In the men's room, Walker came directly to the point. "I wanna roll that goddamn queer."

"I don't know, Walker . . ." Kevin had a lengthy rap sheet, but it included no violent offenses.

"Son of a bitch has all kinds of money," Walker pressed on. "Sports coat that cost $500 if it cost a dime. Season tickets for the Niners. Plus, you see the watch and ring?" Cory wore a diamond pinkie ring and a gold Omega.

"Yeah, but he's decent enough. He bought us drinks—"

"Are you stupid enough to think he did that from the goodness of his heart?" Walker kicked the floor with a boot. "I know how those faggots work. They're nice for one reason, to get their hands on your cock."

"Yeah, but . . ." Kevin still sounded unconvinced.

"But *what?* Watch and ring alone are worth a coupla thou', apart from whatever's in his wallet. Nice payday."

"Well, you put it like that . . ."

"That's exactly how I put it," broke in Walker. And then he laid out the plan.

"We were thinking," said Walker, "you're new to the area, so you probably don't know the good bars. This one's not real exciting. Now me and Kevin, we know 'em all. If you want, we could take you someplace livelier."

"Like where?"

"There's a place on Fifteenth and Adams called Sam's Speakeasy. Lotta people, lotta fun, gets a little wild at times. But there's something you should know. Sometimes you get a lotta gays there. If you ain't comfortable with gays we should go someplace else."

Cory looked Walker in the eye. "That won't be a problem." He signaled for the bill. "How far is it?"

"Seven or eight miles from here. Route's kinda tricky, though. Easiest thing would be to follow us. Is your car out back?" The Emerald's parking lot was behind the building it shared with a bakery and a discount shoe store, both closed for hours. Cory nodded.

"Let's go, then." A minute later, the three of them stood in the parking lot.

"That's mine," said Cory, indicating a silver BMW. "Which one's yours?" Kevin pointed to his pickup.

"Make sure I'm in the rearview mirror, okay? I don't know my way around the city yet."

"Oh, we'll make sure." Walker hit Cory with a right hook that landed on his jaw with a bone-snapping crack, followed by a volley of punches and kicks, so hard and quick that Cory barely had a chance to groan before he fell, crumpled, his breath a bubbling sigh as blood poured from his mouth. In fleeting moments Walker saw him as different people, as Father Flynn and the uncles, every motherfucking one of them, and Rollie Sims and Lieutenant Lorca. He saw him as black and Jewish and Latino, as all the ones he'd hated, the ones who'd kept him down with a foot on his throat. He kicked Cory until his feet hurt.

"Jesus, don't kill the bastard!" Kevin was trying not to panic.

"A few days in the hospital and he'll be fine." Walker pocketed Cory's watch and ring; he took the wallet from Cory's sport coat. "Okay, let's get outta here."

Two days later, Cory died without regaining

consciousness. Walker and Kevin were in custody by then.

At Walker's trial, the jury only deliberated for two hours before finding him guilty. His sentence: life without parole. The strongest witness against him was Kevin Zorn, who copped a plea for conspiracy to commit assault. Kevin's sentence: three years suspended after eighteen months.

XI. LIFE

"There's something I wanna talk about," said Walker as he entered Valentine's office. He was now almost four years into his life sentence.

"All right." Valentine motioned for him to sit.

"It's something I never told no one. Not even Iris." Taking in a deep breath, focusing on the doctor's desktop, he began the story of what had happened with Father Flynn. He spoke for half an hour, dry-eyed, his voice a monotone.

"I'm glad you told me," said Valentine when he finished. "It must have been hard to carry it around for all those years. But I'm curious. What made you decide to talk about it now?"

"Because last night I dreamt about him. Months go by and I don't think about him, but outta nowhere came this dream. Maybe 'cause yesterday I read a *Newsweek* that had an article about the Pope."

"What happened in the dream?"

"It was . . . a reversal, like. See, *he* was the one locked up here. He sat on his bunk in khakis, no collar, and I stood outside his cell. He was mumbling so soft and low that I couldn't hardly understand him. And that was all, a real short dream, didn't last longer than ten seconds."

"What would you do if he came into this room now?"

"I dunno. Maybe pick him up and slam him against the wall. Maybe ask him why he did it. Maybe just sit and look at him. Thing is, he'd be close to eighty. Wouldn't hardly be the same man who did those things. Hell, I dunno."

Walker paused and looked past Valentine. "I wonder what woulda happened if he didn't do what he did. I know he wasn't the only problem. There was Pa dying, and my useless mother, and the uncles. It ain't like my life was a bowl of cherries before he came along. But maybe . . . maybe there's a chance I wouldn't be here." His tone turned brusque. "Waste of time to brood about it. What's done is done."

"Yes and no. No, you can't change what happened, but it's possible to change the impact that it has on you."

"What's that supposed to mean?"

"It means that maybe it won't bother you as much as it does now. You won't forget it, but maybe you'll do a better job of living with it."

"So, maybe I wouldn't hate the son of a bitch as much as I do now?"

"Maybe you wouldn't carry around as much hate as you do now, period."

Walker considered this. "Sometimes I think hate's the only thing that keeps me going here."

"People change, even in a place like this. Maybe other things could keep you going."

"Like what?"

Valentine waited a moment before replying. In fact he often wondered what kept the lifers going. The hope of getting out at sixty-five or seventy? Visits? Religion? Of course, small pleasures were available to them. An above-average meal, a decent book, the World Series or NBA playoffs. The chance to walk outside, on a concrete patio, on an agreeable spring or autumn day. But what precisely could *he* offer them? Medication? An opportunity to air grievances and old traumas? The mixed blessing of insight?

Valentine figured he could do a one-year bid himself, two at most. Anything longer and he'd try his best to find a way to kill himself. Admittedly this made him something of a hypocrite, since they often asked him to treat suicidal inmates.

"I can't answer that," the doctor replied. "It's a question you have to find the answer to yourself. Different people come up with different reasons."

Walker fidgeted in the chair, shifting weight on his wide haunches, leaning slightly forward. He seemed to be carrying on a debate within himself; *how much will I tell him?* Finally: "That man I killed . . . I didn't mean to kill him, not that it matters now. Once I started to hit him, I don't think I coulda stopped, even if a cop was there, a dozen cops. After it happened I felt different. I still had hate in me, but not so much. Thing is, it gets to be a burden. Maybe, as I get older, I'll get rid of more of it. Maybe I'll get rid of it altogether. You never know."

"No, you never do."

For the first time in their twenty-five or so meetings, Valentine felt a fleeting closeness to Walker, not an intimate connection but something akin to it. He contemplated the inmate who sat beside his desk, a hulking neo-Nazi who'd killed a stranger with his fists and feet, his skin coarsened by thousands of cigarettes and vats of booze, his greasy ponytail already flecked with gray. A man well into middle age who might, just might, be beginning to grow tired of life as a hater.

Jesus Christ, he marveled, *I think I can work with him.*

"You never do," repeated Valentine. Walker nodded, barely perceptibly. Their body language loosened as both of them fell back against their chairs.

ONE TO ONE

"IT'S STILL EXPERIMENTAL," said Valentine, the prison psychiatrist. "At least for us. Other places have done it for some time now, but we only started a few months ago." He'd called Sarah to invite her to meet with John Sloat, the man who raped her, now serving twenty-five years.

"You'll be perfectly safe, of course," he went on. "The meetings are one to one, but the room's under constant surveillance. There's closed-circuit TV, and guards will be right outside. You'd have access to a phone with an emergency alarm. Press a button and they'll be there in a flash. You don't even have to lift the receiver."

"Somehow that fails to reassure me."

Her pulse was back to normal; she breathed steadily. When Valentine first identified himself, she thought he called to tell her of Sloat's escape. Her worst fear. "But why? I mean why would I want to see him again? *Him . . .*"

"Because, in facilities where they've done this, they've found it helps the women who've been assaulted. Fewer nightmares, fewer cases of post-traumatic stress disorder. It helps them deal with their sense of violation. In a nutshell, it helps them come to terms with what happened and get on with their lives."

He paused. "There's also evidence that the men, the assailants, have lower rates of recidivism when they're released. Most of them don't see their victims as full-fledged human beings. When they do, they sometimes change."

When they're released. She knew Sloat would get out, eventually. They all did, didn't they? Sooner than later, more likely. Everyone knew prisons were bursting at the seams, with most inmates serving a fraction of their sentences. Sloat's twenty-five years might shrink to ten, or even five. He would get out, a free man, free to stalk again and rape again. Perhaps he'd graduate to killing. But he'd be older and more careful. More apt to avoid detection and arrest.

"I don't know," she said. "When I saw him in the courtroom that last day, the day of his sentencing, a wave of relief came over me. Relief that he was out of my life, at least for a long, long time. It was wonderful . . ." Her relief had been enhanced when they'd moved him to a maximum-security facility after he'd gotten into several fights.

"You needn't decide on the spur of the moment. I don't expect you to. But think about it, and I'll get back to you. Or you can call me." He gave her his number at the prison.

Sarah put down the phone, lit a Doral and paced around the living room. The room, like all the rooms, was small. She didn't care for the apartment, which overlooked a dumpy little plaza with a Mr. Donut, a shoe repair place and a liquor store. Dull gray paint flaked in the bathroom, and at night she lay awake and listened to the *drip-drip-drip* of the kitchen faucet. The super, a shifty-eyed youth with breath that smelled of taco chips and chili dogs, never did the things he promised.

Her old place, on the city's outskirts, had been better. No comparison. Spacious sunny rooms comprised half of a two-family dwelling on a quiet street across from a park. A patio, too, and a broad backyard where she and Brett had cookouts with Mike and Jenny, who lived in the other half of the house. Mike and Jenny owned the house, but she never thought of them as landlords.

They were friends, close to Brett and her in age, quick to share a big bowl of pasta and a bottle of Chianti, quick to join them on an outing to the beach or mountains. Brett was away on a business trip on the day that Sloat attacked her, and they'd stayed up all night with her.

It didn't matter how much she'd enjoyed the old place, or how many outings she'd shared with them; she couldn't live there anymore. The rape outweighed a slew of happy memories, and in the end she had to move.

It was an example of the power Sloat held over her. He'd made her hate a place she'd loved, made her move away from friends. She had no idea how to wrest this power from him.

Sarah stubbed out the Doral, only half of it smoked. She loathed cigarettes—the gasping they caused when she jogged and worked out, the way they worsened her bad sinuses, the reek they left in her long dark hair. She hadn't smoked for three years. Once she made it through the first withdrawal pangs, abstaining had been easy. But one of the cops offered her a Winston the day it happened, and that was that. Since then she'd tried hypnosis, Nicorette gum and patches, to no avail. Her longest stint without a cigarette: nine days.

On top of everything else, she brooded, *he drove me back to smoking.* A smaller voice retorted. *No. You permitted him to make you smoke again. For God's sake, woman, take some responsibility.*

At loose ends, she resumed pacing. It was nearly 10:30, but she was still in a nightie and a bathrobe. She didn't have to work until noon, and she was in no rush to shower and dress. These days she was rarely in a rush to do anything.

She ambled into the kitchen and put on a kettle for instant coffee. Sitting at the table, munching on a two-day-old bagel, she weighed Dr. Valentine's offer. Her first impulse: turn him down. The logistics alone would be too hard to manage. The prison was a ninety-minute drive each way. Apart from the time, driving back and forth would hasten the demise of her Dodge Neon, which already had 80,000 miles on it, and no way could she afford a new car now.

Besides, and more important, seeing Sloat would stir up things she'd tried to bury. What would it accomplish anyway? Valentine said it helped the victims, but did she need help now? Sometimes she went an entire month without a nightmare. She hadn't had a panic attack since a night at the mall eight weeks ago, when a man with a Sloat-like mane of fiery red hair walked behind her in the parking lot.

Victims. The word offended her. She'd grown sick

of labeling herself a victim. Victims lacked control over their lives, a state she found intolerable. In their fights, the most common epithet Brett used to hurl at her had been *control freak.*

But even as she rehashed the reasons for not going, she knew she would. She wanted to see John Sloat locked up, to convince herself that he was really there. Also, she had to admit that she was full of curiosity about him. Just who was he, this brutal stranger who turned her whole world upside down? Why had he done it? How did *he* feel about it?

Who knows, I might even get an apology.

A few minutes later, as she sipped the instant coffee, another thought occurred to her. *Maybe I can figure out a way to kill him.*

To kill John Sloat: an on-and-off fantasy since it had happened. Some days it crossed the line and became a full-blown obsession. She would shoot him, first in the groin, and then work her way up slowly, another bullet in the chest, and finally one in the face, at point-blank range. She'd relish his shock and fear, and she'd pause just long enough before each shot for him to grasp exactly what was happening. Maybe he'd beg for mercy, as she had. To rid the planet of him would be a worthy act, like killing off a water moccasin.

But while she reveled in it, wallowed in it, she'd seen it for what it was: an idle fantasy. They'd held him without bail in the most secure wing of the local jail. At the trial they made everyone pass through a metal detector; they would have spotted a gun or knife in a heartbeat. The case received a good deal of publicity, and cops and marshals swarmed everywhere.

She couldn't kill him in the jail, or in the courtroom, and then he went to prison, and she surely couldn't kill him there. Sarah was not a woman to dwell upon an idle fantasy, and so she let it go. For the most part.

But that was before Valentine's invitation to meet with him, one to one. Perhaps a plan would come to her.

* * *

Sarah sat in a conference room in the part of the prison which housed Mental Health Services—MHS. The room, more inviting than she'd anticipated, had a warm autumnal feel to it. It was done in tan and reddish orange, with dark green trim.

After meeting her at the visitors security check, Valentine took her on a cursory tour of MHS and briefed her in his office. Finally he'd brought her here, where the meeting would take place.

Trying to distract herself, to maintain a focus, she scrutinized the doctor. A heavyset black man of uncertain age; he could have been forty-five or sixty. Nice eyes, trim mustache. Tired. She wondered what it was like for him to work with the likes of Sloat, year in and year out; she wondered what kind of toll it took on him.

"Anything else you want to ask before we bring him in?"

She shook her head.

"Are you ready, then?"

"As ready as I'll ever be." She made a new row of indentations on her Styrofoam coffee cup and willed herself to breathe.

"All right." He rose, gave her shoulder a quick light tap and left her alone in the warm autumnal room. A minute later, he returned with her onetime assailant.

Sloat nodded and sat across from her, resting his folded hands on the table, which was wide enough so they couldn't touch each other, even if they lunged. Meanwhile Valentine stood by the head of the table, between them, like a referee.

"You understand," he addressed them both in his even, measured baritone, "that either of you may end this meeting at any point. The allotted time, if you choose to use it all, is an hour and a quarter. I'll be back then, if not before."

He nodded to them, turned away and left, and Sarah was alone with the man who'd raped her.

She made herself look at him, focusing on details of his appearance as she'd done throughout the trial. A triangular face, coarse pallid skin, receding chin. His most notable feature was a shock of reddish orange hair, almost as bright and garish as Ronald McDonald's. Dark blue eyes, too close together. The eyes, avoiding hers, were sad and glazed now.

Not a handsome man, but not an ugly one. Tall and lanky, about 6'1" or 6'2", weighing no more than 200. A nice enough body, under other circumstances. All in all, a man who could have found himself a woman without resorting to . . . *that* . . .

She kept on looking at him, holding her silence, trying to desensitize herself to him. *There's nothing he can do to me. I'm safe now. All I have to do is press the button.* Slowly, discretely, she slid her hand towards it.

"Well. Here we are." Her voice rang flat and stilted. The voice of a woman she didn't know, the voice of a robot equipped with skillfully programmed but not quite human speech.

"Yes'm. Here we are." His tone, polite and mild; the *Yes'm* threw her for a loop. Again, she fell silent.

While driving to the prison, Sarah had considered various opening gambits. *Tell me, how does it feel to be the powerless one now? I hope they do to you what you did to me. I hope that every hour, every minute of your sentence is a misery for you.* She'd also considered spitting in his face.

Now, as she sat across from him, the gambits dissolved into irrelevance. The rage would have to stay inside her, unvented, a while longer. Too soon to relinquish it. Instead, she asked him, "What's it like here?"

The question seemed to surprise him. "You mean, what's a typical day here like?"

"Yes. A typical day."

"Lessee. We get up at 6:10 if we want breakfast. Many guys don't bother with it, they'd rather sleep. Then we shower, four at a time. That can take a good chunk of the morning. Then we go to work, those of us with jobs. Lunch is early, 11:05 . . ." He went through the rest of the day's minutiae. The times for rec and commissary, the times when they might go to sick call or classes or AA meetings, the empty hours in their cells.

"It sounds incredibly boring."

"It is."

"Good."

She opened her purse, took out a pack of Dorals and lit a cigarette without offering him one. "What's your cell like?"

"About what you'd expect. Six by ten. Bunk beds riveted to the floor. Sink without a stopper, stainless steel toilet without a lid. We share a shelf, where we keep our books and stuff."

"How many to a cell?"

"On my tier, two. Varies, tier to tier. Roberto Santos, he's my cellie. Snores something fierce, used to snort a lot of coke and it messed up the inside of his nose, but he's okay. I coulda done worse."

"What's he in for?"

"They said he had a, uhm, relationship with his second cousin when she was thirteen. He showed me a picture of her. She sure doesn't *look* like a thirteen-year-old."

"How old is he?"

"Thirty."

Sarah bristled. "So it's okay if a man of thirty has sex with a girl of thirteen as long as she looks older?"

The blue eyes flashed. "Now wait, I never said that."

"It's what you implied."

"Look, you asked me what he was in for and I told you. The rest of it was conversation."

Her anger ebbed, and she paused before she spoke again. "Maybe this whole thing is a bad idea," she said with a sigh she tried to mute. "I never should have come." She wanted to be in her apartment, or at work, or even at the health club on the treadmill, her least favorite exercise machine. She wanted to be anywhere except in this room, with this man.

He took a generic cigarette from the pocket of his khaki prison shirt and played with it before he lit it. "Why don't you tell me something about yourself?"

"Like what?"

"Like, uhm, where you're from. What your family's like. Ordinary stuff." His voice was almost pleasant. Completely different from the way it was that day: guttural, unyielding, hard and cold as a hammer hitting metal. Barking out orders, one hand holding a sawed-off shotgun. *Do like I say and I won't kill you. Take off your clothes, real slow, no quick moves. Okay, we're going to the bedroom now . . .*

She sighed again. "I'm from Kentucky. Louisville. It's a small family, my parents and me and a younger sister. We moved here when I was eleven. My father's company transferred him. At college I studied art history."

"That must have been interesting, art history."

"Yes, but not too practical. I've worked in a framing

shop since I graduated. That was five years ago." *Jesus Christ, I don't believe it! Here I am, making small talk with this asshole, telling him about my life as though we're on a blind date!*

"I used to like art too. My best subject. I wanted to be an artist when I grew up."

"What happened?"

He shrugged. "My mom went kinda crazy, and she and my dad split. We hadda go on State. I, uhm, lost interest."

She raised her eyebrows. "Your mother went crazy?"

"Uh huh. Coupla times she got so bad they sent her to the loony bin."

"What was she like when she went crazy?"

He lit another cigarette from the butt of the first one; ashes dotted the table. With both of them smoking, an acrid cloud was taking form. "Lessee, it's been awhile. Well, she used to get real suspicious about the neighbors. She believed they tried to gas us when we slept, like they had some kinda diabolical power over us. The devil was always a real big thing to her. She used to purge us, because she thought the devil lived inside us."

"Purge you?"

He blushed. "She, uhm, she gave us these enemas, see. Two or three in a row. Sometimes we wouldn't make it to the toilet in time, and then she beat on us because we made a mess."

Sarah felt a short-lived surge of sympathy for him in spite of herself. "So," she responded deliberately, "you know what it's like to be at someone's mercy. To lack control completely."

For the first time he looked at her directly, without blinking. "Yes'm, I sure do. I know that feeling real well." She returned his steady gaze in kind.

The rest of the time passed quickly. She described growing up in Louisville. He knew nothing about Kentucky except they had some kind of big horse race there. On his part, he described life in the projects, which he described as often rougher than it was in prison. They spoke a bit more about their families—guardedly, gingerly.

When Valentine came in, precisely an hour and a quarter after they'd begun, she looked surprised. It didn't seem that that much time had passed.

He asked if they wanted to meet again. They did.

Driving home, mulling over their encounter, Sarah was struck by three things. First: her failure to express her anger, still torrential, still bottled up inside her. She'd always assumed that, if given the chance, she'd yell at him, scream at him, belittle him. Try to make him feel like the lowest cockroach who ever crawled across the earth. But she hadn't. She hadn't used the mildest profanity, not once. In fact she'd barely raised her voice. She recounted how soft-spoken she'd been, and it made her want to throw up.

Second: neither of them had mentioned the rape itself. A few times she'd referred to it, obliquely and in passing, but that was all. She made a vow. The *next* time she would bring it up, without fail.

Third: she still wanted to kill him.

*   *   *

Sarah walked alone in a park, or maybe a cemetery. The night was dark and unmistakably ominous. Suddenly she heard footsteps coming from behind her. She turned around, saw no one, but she knew he was there, stalking her, playing cat and mouse with her, biding his time. She walked faster but the footsteps followed suit.

She started to run. Sweat poured off her despite the damp cold night. She turned around again. This time she could see him. It was too dark to make out details of his face but she knew it was him, of course it was, who else could it be? She ran faster. Tripped. When she fell, he threw himself on top of her. She lay there, immobilized—paralyzed. She breathed in loud, anguished gasps. He pried her legs apart with a knee. She tried to scream, but he covered her mouth with his hand.

As usual, she woke up drenched and moaning.

She bolted out of bed and turned the light on. Baseball bat in hand—she slept with it propped against her bedside table—she looked beneath the bed and inside the closet. Then she checked the rest of the apartment. Everywhere, including behind the love seat wedged against her living room wall, and in the tiny recess between her fridge and stove. Places where no man could possibly conceal himself. A senseless ritual, she knew, but she couldn't give it up.

Satisfied that no one else was there, she opened the fridge and poured herself a glass of milk. Her hand shook as she held the carton. *It's been months since I had one that bad.*

She drained the glass, sat down at the kitchen table. The fear turned to fury. At first the object of her wrath was Valentine. Who the fuck did he think he was, this quack with his bright idea of shoving them together? And just when she had started to get over it, when what she wanted most was to be left alone. Valentine was a shrink; supposedly he knew about emotions. Did he know what this meeting of theirs had cost her, how much it had set her back?

The rage veered away from Valentine and toward its customary target. And, as it mounted, as it fed on itself, her old obsession returned full force. *How could I kill him? How?*

Drumming her fingers on the kitchen table, she tried to approach his murder coolly, like an algebra problem. The metal detector ruled out gun, knife and most blunt instruments. She could bring him some poisoned food or beverage. Tricky, though. What kind would she use? Where would she get it, anyway? It wasn't as if she could go to K-Mart and ask where they kept the poisons. Besides, he'd be suspicious. *Here, John, all is forgiven, have a cyanide brownie.* She didn't like the idea of poison anyway. Too genteel. It reminded her of a British mystery on Public Television.

Was there a way to give him AIDS? Now *there* was an appealing notion. AIDS would kill him slowly, with suitable suffering beforehand. He might go blind or crazy, or end up paralyzed and incontinent. He might develop those grotesque skin cancers, Kaposi's sarcomas. Sarah knew a fair bit about AIDS. She'd read up on it while she waited for results of her blood test after he raped her.

The notion was as absurd as it was appealing. All she had to do was get hold of tainted bodily fluids and then figure out a way to get it into his bloodstream.

How to kill someone, painfully, in a tightly monitored setting, with no suspicious metallic device of any kind? She tried to sift through whodunits she'd read since her teens, through hours of watching Perry Mason and Colombo and their ilk. Distractedly, she reached across the table for her cigarettes. A cheap plastic lighter lay next to it.

Lighter fluid.

She picked up the lighter, contemplated it, shook it, smiled at it. The plan, which came to her fully formed, was close to foolproof. She would collect enough to douse him, bring it to the prison in her purse, and throw it in his face and on his clothes as she sat across from him. Ignite it—

Probably wouldn't kill him, though. Guards would rush in and save his life. But that was okay too. He'd still be badly burned. With luck, disfigured. The treatment, skin grafts and whatnot, were notoriously painful.

Lighter fluid. Cheap, obtainable everywhere. It would pass through a metal detector as easily as cotton candy. Sarah felt excited and a bit frightened. This one, unlike her other fantasies, was plausible. She could do it if she wanted to. *If.*

Most likely she'd have to spend some time in prison herself. Maybe not. A good lawyer might get her off, despite her unarguable guilt. Sarah, like most people with firsthand exposure to the criminal justice system, regarded it cynically. If Sloat had had the money for some slick shyster who charged $400 per hour, he'd be free now. She didn't doubt it for a minute.

But what if she did end up in prison? Sarah, a law-abiding sort, had no experience with legal trouble more serious than speeding tickets. She'd barely *broken* any laws. In college she smoked pot, no more than half a dozen times: the full extent of her use of drugs. She hadn't even bothered to get a fake ID. So, how would she—a model citizen, something of a goody-goody—cope with incarceration? The fact was, prison terrified her. Confinement, hundreds of restrictions . . . stultifying boredom . . . constant menace, unwelcome sexual advances. She knew what it was like now. Visiting Sloat had made it real.

I guess I'll have to decide if it's worth it to me.

Lighting a cigarette, regarding the lighter fondly, she considered other details. She could transfer the lighter fluid to a different container. The can had a plastic nozzle with a tiny opening. If she used one, it would take too long to soak him. A jar would be better.

A small jar with a broad mouth and a lid that came off easily.

A jar of cold cream, emptied out and cleaned.

She ran into the bathroom, almost skipping, opened the medicine cabinet and took out the cold cream. The opaque glass would conceal the fluid within it, the cover would come off with one quick twist. Perfect.

Too excited to sit still now, she paced from room to room as the scenario unfolded. She'd sit across from him, her purse on the table. She'd reach inside, ostensibly for cigarettes. Instead, she'd find the jar, pull it out, unscrew the cover and throw the contents onto him. Then she'd grab a book of matches, strike them, throw them at him. She'd soak the matches in lighter fluid beforehand for good measure.

She could practice the whole thing over and over, until the sequence was automatic. The more she practiced, the faster and more smoothly she could do it. In time she might get it down to less than a second. Much too short a time for him to protect himself or for anyone to stop her.

She smiled as she imagined his astonishment and then his terror, his pupils wide as saucers, his screaming and helplessness. Above all else, his helplessness.

*   *   *

"I want to talk about what you did to me," Sarah opened, her brownish-green eyes boring into him. Their second meeting had just begun.

"Okay." Sloat's face looked drawn and wary.

"Do you remember, or were you too drugged up?"

"I remember bits and pieces of it. Some of it's kinda hazy on account of booze and coke."

"Let me fill you in. You waited in the park one morning until my boyfriend and the next-door neighbors left. Then you crossed the street and rang the bell. You said you were from UPS. I opened the door and you lunged inside. You swung at me, hit me full force in the face and knocked me down. When I fell, you threw yourself on top of me, covering my mouth. You took the gun from your knapsack. First, you held it under my chin, then against my ear. Are you with me so far?"

He nodded, blinking often.

"You told me to take off my clothes." She spoke in the same deliberate fashion as before, but now her tone had a clipped, accusing edge. "We went into the bedroom. You walked behind me. One hand had me in a hammerlock, the other held the gun. Once we got there, you hit me again, in the ribs. Did I mention that you hit me hard enough to knock a tooth out? By the way, why *did* you hit me that second time? I did exactly what you told me to. Because I was crying? Did that offend you?"

"No, Ma'am, I don't think so—"

"Goddamn you, stop calling me *Ma'am!* How *dare* you call me that! *Ma'am* is a term of respect, or haven't you heard? *Ma'am* is what they call the frigging Queen of England!" For the first time, she was yelling at him.

"What do you want me to call you? Sarah?"

"Don't call me *anything!* As far as you're concerned I have no name, okay? Anyway, isn't that how you'd prefer it? If I have no name, I'm not a real person, so it doesn't matter what you did to me."

"It matters." There was a hint of sadness in his voice. Not quite remorse, but sadness. Maybe she was just imagining it.

She paused to light a cigarette and blew a smoke ring towards the ceiling. "Let's see," she resumed, "where were we? The bedroom, yes. You hit me in the ribs. When I was still on the floor, you loosened your belt and unzipped your fly. Tell me if I'm leaving out things—" She went on to recount the balance of the morning, and all the time she looked at him, unyielding and unflinching.

When she finished, it was the better part of a minute before she spoke again. "What I want to know . . . well, there are a lot of things I want to know, but what I want to know, more than anything else, is how you felt. What exactly did you get from it?"

Framing an answer, he rubbed his temples as if trying to dispel a headache. "There was . . . there was an excitement to it. I don't like admitting it, but it's the truth. I'm learning to respect the truth, that's something new for me. And anger comes into it, I always been carrying around so much of it. Not just towards women but toward everyone."

Again, he rubbed his temples. "There's something else," he said when he resumed. "What I did, it was like something that I had to do. I don't expect you to understand it. Hell, I don't understand it real well myself."

"Something you had to do. Why?"

"For . . . for the release."

"For the release. You raped me, and ruined your own life in the bargain, let's not forget—you did that for *release*?" She emitted a joyless laugh. "Jesus, man, did you ever hear of masturbation?"

"I, uhm, . . . see, uhm, I don't hardly ever do that," he stammered. To her amazement, his face reddened deeply. He'd beaten her, disrobed her at gunpoint, forced himself on her, yet the mention of masturbation left him nearly incoherent.

For once she was too taken aback to be angry with him. "Why not, for Christ's sake?"

He lit a cigarette, unsteadily, trying to pull himself together. "Mom, uhm, never had much use for sex. It was dirty, it was wrong, and that was all there was to it. She never went out with other men after Dad left, even though she was still young and not too bad to look at neither. My brothers and me, we used to wonder how we got to be born at all. We used to joke about virgin birth."

He puffed on the cigarette in small quick drags. "Well, when I was twelve or so, I began to grow up, to have a grown man's body. And I'd, uhm, you know, touch myself . . . masturbate." He pronounced it hurriedly, *mas'bate,* as if the word polluted him. "Well, to make a long story short, she caught me at it once."

"What did she do?"

"She went crazy. Spent an hour ranting about the devil and quoting the Bible, about that dude who spilled his seed on the floor of his tent and how God struck him dead. Then she left, real sudden. I thought she was finished but she wasn't. She came back with a bread knife. She held it against my, uhm, you know, my private parts. And she promised me, in the name of God Almighty, that she'd cut it off if she ever caught me at it again."

He paused. Beads of sweat had formed across his forehead. "Well, I guess that's why I don't, uhm, mas'bate too much."

Another pause. "I'm sorry," Sarah said finally. "I'm sorry your mother was so crazy. But it still gives you no right to do what you did to me. You had no right, *no right*—" She fought back tears.

"There comes a point," she went on, more calmly, "when you're responsible for what you do, regardless of what's been done to you." As she spoke, she thought of the jar of cold cream in the purse beside her. This time it only contained cold cream. She brought it as a test, to see if they'd open it when she passed through security. They didn't.

"You may not believe I mean this, but I agree with you."

They fell silent, and Sarah studied him with a cold detachment. "How do you feel about women?" she asked him.

He seemed to expect the question. "Valentine keeps askin' me that too. Guess he thinks I hate them all, on account of my mother was so crazy. Well, maybe he's right but I doubt it. There were women I liked, who were good to me. One aunt in particular, Aunt Phyllis. She used to read me stories and stuff like that. And there were teachers who knew things at home were kinda tough, and they tried to go the extra mile for me. But the thing is, I didn't know too many other girls or women. Didn't have sisters, just brothers. Didn't go out with them much. Didn't go out with them at all till I left home."

"Why not?"

He shook his head. "Mom wouldn't hear of it."

Sarah inhaled deeply. This time she'd come with a clear agenda and she intended to go ahead with it. "I want to tell you how what you did affected me," she resumed. "Let's start with right after you left the house."

She glanced at her watch, noting that she only had fourteen minutes left. Succinctly, she told him of the initial shock . . . the police interrogation, the trip to the ER . . . the weeks when she couldn't stand being alone. The four or five showers she took each day (they'd dropped to two now) . . . the way her mind wandered; how, at first, she couldn't make it through the morning paper. The pulling away from friends and acquaintances. Brett's leaving . . .

That seemed to pique his interest more than anything. "Who's Brett?"

"My boyfriend. Ex-boyfriend."

"How long were you with him?"

"A long time. Ever since my junior year of college. We started to live together when I graduated."

"Why'd he go?"

She stared at him through narrowed pupils. "He couldn't deal with what happened. That's exactly what he said the day he left. *I'm sorry, Sarah, I just can't deal with it.* He stayed with me through the trial, but we both knew that it was over. Towards the end we didn't sleep together, we barely talked. I guess he thought I was used goods or something. Or maybe he thought I wanted it, and you were my idea of fun."

"He was a jerk. You're better off without him."

Her mouth dropped open. "I beg your pardon!"

"You heard me." He spoke with unmistakable conviction. "You're better off without him."

She was almost too angry to speak. "How *dare* you . . . *you*, of all people!"

He leaned toward her. "This may surprise you, but I know things about right and wrong. And it's wrong to leave someone who's going through a real bad time. It was wrong for my dad to leave my mom when she started to go off the deep end, and it was wrong for what's-his-name to leave you on account of me. A man who cared about you woulda hung around."

She said nothing more until Valentine appeared a minute or so later. Instead, she looked at Sloat with an iota of grudging agreement. She couldn't argue with him, since she'd reached the same conclusion about Brett herself.

That night she dreamt of Sloat again. The dream, short and simple, consisted of little more than a few images. He lay powerless in the middle of a bed, trying to hide beneath a sheet. A woman stood by the side of the bed, immobile, a knife in her hand. Sarah herself stood on the opposite side of the bed, arms crossed, silent.

The woman with the knife ignored her. She heard a sound, a whimper, coming from the bed.

She woke up, but she fell back to sleep in an instant. The next morning it occurred to her that she'd finally dreamt about him and it hadn't been a nightmare. Not a pleasant dream, but not a nightmare.

*   *   *

If my heart doesn't stop this pounding, she told herself, *I'll die before I get there.* She was ten miles from the prison, en route to their fourth meeting. Her purse was next to her. In addition to the usual—wallet, cigarettes, a roll of Certs, makeup—it contained an opaque glass jar full of lighter fluid and a book of specially soaked matches.

She used an old trick to distract herself, a trick she'd devised in college. She'd conjure up images of certain paintings and immerse herself in them. Almost a form of self-hypnosis. Monet's *Water Lilies* worked best.

The old trick worked, and she felt more relaxed as the remaining miles sped by. She'd only made a few trips to the prison but they were already becoming routine. Parking, outside the fences topped with curlicues of razor-sharp barbed wire. Smiling, as she made her way through security, where some of the guards now recognized her; one of them had begun to flirt a bit. Signing in; having someone from MHS come out to escort her. A cup of muddy, bitter coffee while she waited for them to bring in Sloat.

This time, he spoke first. "I, uhm, got something," he began shyly. "I asked Valentine if it was okay for me to show it to you and he said it was."

"Oh?"

"It's a drawing. See, I've started to draw a bit again."

He reached down, picked up a piece of paper from the desk. It was a sketch of a bunch of flowers, red and purple, done in colored pencils. The flowers, tulips, filled a vase which sat on top of a wooden table.

She looked it over carefully, trying to frame an appropriate response. "Not bad," she offered judgment. She meant it. Balanced composition, an obvious attention to detail. Skillful use of shading, of light and shadow. Despite the bright flowers, the drawing conveyed a melancholy, especially in its indigo background.

"Not bad," she repeated. "You made a simple drawing but you captured a lot of feeling in it."

"You can keep it if you'd like."

She shook her head briskly. "I don't think so!" There were limits.

"Okay."

She handed the drawing back to him, flummoxed. *He tries to give me a sketch of tulips while I'm intending to douse him in lighter fluid.*

"I assume you have no flowers in your cell. How'd you do it without a subject?"

"I took out a book on flowers from the library. Something about the tulips caught my eye. Always liked flowers, not that I saw too many of them growing up."

He hesitated. "You know that park, across from where you used to live? I'd go there every chance I could to walk around the gardens."

"I suppose"—she reached into her purse, took a cigarette and held it, unlit—"I suppose that's where you noticed me. In the park."

He nodded. "Nearly every day you used to run there. Same time, same path."

"Such consistency. I must have been a rapist's dream."

He said nothing.

"How long did you stalk me?"

"Couple of weeks. Maybe more."

The old rage, fractionally lessened when he showed her the drawing, returned full force. "A couple of weeks, maybe more. Time enough for you to chart my every move. Time to follow me and find out where I lived. Time to learn when Brett was there and when he wasn't. Time to plan it out in every detail."

Again, he said nothing.

Still holding the unlit cigarette, she reached inside her purse again with her free hand, ostensibly to find a book of matches. Instead, she touched the lid of the opaque glass jar. One quick twist, followed by a little toss. She loosened the lid (it loosened easily), and felt around for the book of treated matches. She could do it, right then, on the spot.

He sat across from her, waiting, his dark blue eyes wary. But they were often wary. It didn't mean he knew that she was up to something.

A thought dawned on her, as sharp as a blast of cold air on a hot summer day—*I needn't do this now if I don't want to.* Ignoring him, she turned her eyes towards the ceiling while she gave the new thought play. She could do it now, or a week from now, or any point throughout their remaining meetings. Or, she could wait until his release and do it then, when he least expected it.

Or she could choose not to. She could grant him the clemency he'd denied her. Forego the notion of a violent retribution, which she didn't quite approve of, despite its obvious attractiveness. But either way it would be her choice, hers alone.

A wave of relief passed through her, even balmier than the wave of relief she'd known when they had sentenced him. *I needn't do it now if I don't want to. It will be my choice, and mine alone. I will be the judge and jury.*

For the first time since John Sloat had assaulted her—it might have been a lifetime ago—Sarah felt empowered. She felt her posture change; she sat up a bit straighter; she felt the tension in her back and shoulders lessen. That night, when she went back to her apartment, she'd put away the baseball bat. And she felt she was ready to try again to quit smoking. This time she could do it; she was sure of it.

THE STEPHEN HAWKING DEATH ROW FAN CLUB

CASE WAS THE PRISON'S SENIOR SOCIAL WORKER, a thin man of thirty-eight with vague blue eyes and a reddish-brown beard already flecked with gray. An apologetic aura clung to him. *Excuse me for taking up your time, for breathing so much of your oxygen.*

"It makes no sense . . ." he argued mildly.

"Bureaucrats don't have to make no sense," said Valentine, his boss. Herbert Valentine, a light-skinned black man, a fifty-four-year-old psychiatrist, directed the prison's mental health services. For reasons Case could never fathom, the doctor was prone to making intentional grammatical errors despite majoring in

English at Dartmouth before he went to medical school. Heavy-set, with a pencil-thin mustache that stretched above tight lips, he reminded Case of Raymond, the constipated hero of the Milk of Mag TV ads from the 1980s.

"It's not like we've got all the manpower in the world," Case pressed on. "We've got 688 inmates and a mental health of staff of seven."

"I'm aware of the stats."

Case blushed briefly—*I'm not implying that you weren't.* He fidgeted as he sat in front of Valentine's desk, crossing and uncrossing his legs.

"But regular rounds on Death Row will take a full day each month. More, with the paperwork."

"Bullshit. Ain't no one askin' you to psychoanalyze 'em, Case. See each of 'em once a month for fifteen or twenty minutes, write notes and you're done by lunch. Hell, we only got four of 'em. It's not like we're Florida or Texas." They lived in a small state with deeply mixed feelings about capital punishment. The population backed it three to one, but no one had actually been put to death since Eisenhower's second term.

Valentine looked at him over the top of his half-glasses. "You ever been to Death Row?" Case shook his head.

"Interesting. Eight or nine years you been here, and you haven't set foot there. Why not?"

He shrugged. "I had enough to do on the other blocks. It seemed like a waste to spend time with a handful of guys they want to kill anyway. And even if they get their sentences overturned, they're almost certain to be lifers. I'd rather work with the ones who'll be getting out."

"Were you afraid to go there?"

"I don't think so." Case blushed again. He glanced outside, through one of the narrow windows in Valentine's office. A dozen inmates stood around in the rec yard, clustered in groups of three or four beneath a gunmetal sky.

"There're lawsuits brought by Death Row inmates in other states petitioning for more services, including regular visits from mental health personnel," resumed Valentine. "The bureaucrats want to reduce the chances for litigation here. It's that simple."

"But—"

Valentine fixed him with a look that said *Don't argue with me, Peckerwood.* "Just see 'em. All of 'em, once a month, beginning today. I left their charts on your desk."

*   *   *

The bleakness of his office weighed on Case more than usual as he sat in his torn vinyl desk chair, the Death Row inmates' charts in front of him. His office was like Valentine's, only smaller, a cinder block cubicle filled with derelict furniture and dented filing cabinets. A slit of a window gave him a view of the rec yard bounded by barbed wire. The cinder block walls made it almost impossible to hang things but he'd managed to affix a calendar from the National Wildlife Federation to a bulletin board. The calendar provided the office's only splash of color. This month featured a red-eyed tree frog from Costa Rica.

Case picked up the first chart. Thelmore Higgins, black male aged thirty-six, on Death Row ten years and two months for the murder of Sheila Newman. He abducted her one night in the parking lot as she left a video store, knocked her out with the butt of his .38, threw her into the back of his car, drove to the country, and raped her in a cornfield. He shot her in the lower abdomen at point-blank range, turning most of her pelvic organs into pulp. But she didn't die immediately. According to the Medical Examiner, she may have lived as long as half an hour while she tried to crawl back to the road, inch by inch.

Welfare mother in and out of prison herself until her mid-thirties; drug dealer father who left a few months after he was born; intractable behavior since age six. He showed athletic promise, especially in football, until dropping out of school in the eleventh grade. IQ of 119, never used for constructive purposes. His two-page rap sheet listed a slew of offenses from shoplifting to first degree sexual assault. Since the age of twenty-one, his longest time out had been eighteen months. No mental health history of any kind.

Case picked up the second chart. Brian Ottway, white male aged forty-six. On Death Row nine years and eleven months. A Death Row rarity, a college graduate. He'd even attained a modest prosperity as the owner of a small bookstore, which did all right before Barnes & Noble and Amazon.com. About to go broke, drinking a pint or two of cheap brandy daily, he shot his wife and five-year-old twin sons with a hunting rifle. They said it had been premeditated because he'd bought a box of shells the day before. Tried to hang himself afterwards but too drunk to get the noose right, he was still farting around with it when the cops arrived.

Solid background by prison standards. His father was a Greyhound Bus driver, his mother a high school lunchroom supervisor. His brother a landscaper, his sister a nurse. IQ of 111. Apart from DWIs, he had no record prior to the murders. Long history of depression, some hints of a bipolar disorder. Had taken various drugs, including three Prozacs a day, but he'd refused all meds since his sentencing. The only Death Row inmate to waive appeals.

Case picked up the third chart. Samuel Marrero, Hispanic male aged twenty-three, on Death Row one year and five months. Three brothers, all incarcerated. He'd begun to drink at age nine, to use marijuana a year later, and heroin two years after that. Supported his habits by burglaries and armed robberies. In the course of sticking up a convenience store he got twitchy and shot the attendant in the head three times. He also shot the only witness, a woman who came in to buy orange juice.

Seventh grade education. Illiterate, with an IQ of 78. Hadn't helped himself in court by smirking, yelling, and giving the finger to the State's Attorney at the end of her summation. On-again, off-again mental health contact, mainly in jails and prison—plagued by drug flashbacks and the voices of dead relatives. He'd been on Thorazine, Haldol and lithium, as well as less potent medications. Psychological testing indicated brain damage, mainly from childhood beatings. One of them had landed him in an ICU for two weeks with a fractured skull.

Case picked up the fourth chart. Jesse Wayne Arnott, black male aged twenty-eight, on Death Row three years and one month. While serving time for auto theft, he and a cellie had tried to escape. They held a CO hostage, and Arnott was convicted of stabbing him with an eight-inch shank. The cellie pled guilty, accepted twelve years, and turned out to be the chief witness against him. Arnott always held that the cellie himself had been the killer. The shank, in fact, showed both sets of fingerprints.

High school graduate, IQ of 102. No memories of his biological parents—never knew his father, abandoned by his mother. Raised by his paternal grandparents until they arrested the grandfather for sexually assaulting him. Used to take Tegretol for flashbacks from the sexual abuse.

Case jotted down a few notes, took a last glance outside, and left for Death Row.

Most of the cell blocks were raucous places, filled with a din of yelling, of unwatched TVs blaring and an unintelligible PA system, of steel doors clanging. A din that picked up strength, like a hurricane moving across the open sea, as it swept along the corridors. Anticipating the usual sound and fury, Case was jolted by the Death Row ambiance, as quiet as an empty church. It held eight cells, four of them uninhabited. On Death Row, in contrast to almost all the other housing units, every inmate had a single cell.

At the end of the corridor was a visiting room, windowless and bare except for a plastic chair on either side of a wobbly desk. Escorted by a CO, Case glanced across the room. He noticed right away: no phone. Prison phones almost always had panic buttons which could summon a swarm of all available officers in seconds. Case had never used one, but he liked having them around.

The CO stood next to him, trying to abort a yawn. "Which one you want?"

"I guess I'll start with Higgins."

Well over six feet tall, weighing about 250, as solid as an NFL linebacker, Thelmore Higgins dwarfed the CO who accompanied him. Contrary to Hollywood's version of Death Row, they didn't handcuff inmates here. Case's first thought: *the man could snap my neck like a dry twig.* The CO left, and the room became much smaller. Most of it was occupied by the glaring Higgins.

"Hello." Case pointed to the empty chair. "Sit down."

"Been sittin' all day. I'd rather stand."

"Sit down anyway."

The glare intensified but Higgins sat.

"My name is Duane Case. I'm with Mental Health Services."

"So I figured."

"Really?"

"You hadda be. You ain't one of my lawyers, and you don't look like a preacher, and we ain't related. Not too many other possibilities." The glare moved to Case's face. "What do you want?"

"To see how you're doing. How you're getting along here."

Higgins's laugh sounded like a cross between a bark and cough. "How'm I doin'? I'm locked up twenty-three hours a day waitin' for some racist crackers to give me a lethal injection. Shee-it, I'm doin' fine. Couldn't be much better."

"You're here because of race?"

"Show me a white man on Death Row anywhere, anytime, for killin' a black woman. You do that and I'll say I ain't here because of race."

Case fought back a rejoinder. *Maybe you're on Death Row because you kidnapped a woman, raped her and killed her in an especially heinous manner.* "How do you pass the time?" he asked instead.

"I read, I write letters. Do push-ups and deep knee bends. I wanna be in shape, see, when they kill me. Oh, and I jerk off a lot. Sometimes I play chess with Ottway. The big events are eatin' and sleepin'. Especially sleepin'."

For want of a better question: "How do you get along with Ottway?"

"He's okay, for a white trash piece of shit. Ain't none of us saints here, but at least we didn't kill our own people. He's smart enough to play chess with, which is all I care about. Not lookin' for a bosom buddy."

They fell silent. Glancing around the windowless room, Case felt as great a degree of isolation as he'd ever known. Death Row was not only cut off from the rest of the world, it was cut off from the rest of the prison.

"Do you get visitors?"

"Once in a while."

"Who?"

"Oprah, the president, the pope." The same laugh, part bark and part cough. "Who you think?"

"I have no idea. I didn't check your visiting list."

He shifted on his haunches. "My mother and

stepfather still come, and my brother. Every couple of months I'll see one of my lawyers. That's about it."

Another silence. "You must be carrying around a lot of anger," Case said finally.

"More than you could imagine in your wildest dreams."

The interview staggered on for another fifteen minutes. Higgins talked about his trial, and how the public defender screwed him, and how everyone knew the judge was the state's biggest bigot, and about a Florida case in the 1940s when a black man went to the chair for raping a white woman although she practically admitted that she'd asked him for sex. The jury foreman admitted it too, but he said they wanted to teach the poor bastard a lesson anyway.

He never mentioned his victim, or his previous incarcerations, or his own contributions to his present circumstances. Showed no remorse.

The interview with Jesse Wayne Arnott went better. His unlined face and adolescent manner belied his age; Jesse Wayne looked more like an eighteen-year-old candidate for an inner city job corps than for Death Row.

They talked about Jesse Wayne's case, and the current status of his appeal, but mainly they talked about his life before prison. His first suicide attempt, at fifteen (aspirin, gin and his grandmother's Xanax). His flashbacks. A childhood birthday, the day of the Bicentennial, when they took him to New York to see the Tall Ships and the fireworks: his favorite memory.

Samuel Marrero was short and bent, with coarse sallow skin, his small dark eyes hidden behind thick glasses. The only Death Row inmate who took meds now, for his voices, he walked with a slow stiff gait, a classic Thorazine shuffle. He expressed no curiosity about Case's visit and no interest in the questions, to which he gave only the briefest answers. Yeah, he slept all right; and yeah, his spirits were holding up okay; and yeah, he guessed the medicine helped; and naw, he hadn't heard from his lawyer lately. Case wondered if he cared whether or not they killed him.

The interview with Ottway was the shortest. Case started to introduce himself, but Ottway cut him off with a wave of the hand. "I don't want to talk to you, or any other mental health type. I don't want to talk about my childhood, or my dreams, or whether my mom was mean to me. I'm not interested in insight, rehabilitation or redemption. What I want is to be left alone until they strap me to the gurney, which I wish they'd do today."

He stood up and strode towards the door. Just before he left, he turned to Case. "Have a nice day."

*   *   *

Case came back to Death Row a month later. Higgins called him part of the white racist establishment, and Arnott cried at one point, and Marrero strung together a couple of three-word sentences, and Ottway told him to "stay out of my face, you do-gooding motherfucker." Case returned to his office, wrote notes and brought the charts to Valentine, who motioned for him to sit. "How are you making out down there?"

"I wouldn't call it my favorite place."

"Can you can get anywhere with any of them?"

"I don't know. With Arnott, maybe. So far he's pretty open with me."

Valentine pushed his chair back and rested his feet on the edge of the desk, a gesture of rare informality. "You keep at it, Case. I want that boy to be a model of mental health by the time they stick that needle into him."

The morning of Case's third trip to Death Row was bleak and gray, with chill winds and heavy rain. He began with Higgins, as usual. No special reason, except to get him out of the way. Higgins was his least favorite of the four. He disliked him even more than Ottway, whom he planned to skip anyway, despite Valentine's instructions.

A perfunctory *How've you been?* Higgins's set reply, *Shee-it, I couldn't be much better.* A routine query about his appeal, followed by his routine diatribe about racism. But the diatribe had a *pro forma* quality; it lacked bite.

Ten minutes into their meeting, Higgins looked directly at him, without a glare for once. "I need stuff to read. Most of what they got on that book cart ain't worth the paper it's printed on. Stupid westerns and romances with missin' pages, five-year-old issues of *National Geographic.*"

"What kind of stuff did you have in mind?"

Higgins considered. "Well, I was always curious about *The Autobiography of Malcolm X.* And I like James Baldwin. But what I'd like most is *A Brief History of Time.*"

Case coughed in surprise. "What's the matter, Case?" asked Higgins with a withering scowl. "You can't believe I'd be interested in a book like that?"

"No, but it's not the kind of reading material that's popular here."

"You read it?"

"As a matter of fact, I have."

Had it not been for the basic sciences, Case would most likely have gone to medical school. A good student in English, history, sociology and the like, he foundered in introductory chemistry and physics. He did not possess the kind of mind that was intrigued by how a toaster worked, or a pancreas or kidney. Majoring in psychology, he earned a graduate degree in social work and forgot about medicine, more or less. His indifference to science remained with him. No branch of it sparked his interest, with one exception: cosmology.

Cosmology, the study of the universe as a whole, its origins and its expansion and its fate. Cosmology, which addressed the questions which had haunted him as a child. How could there be a beginning of the universe, but how could there not be? What lay beyond the edge of it? How could there *be* an edge of it—again, how could there not be? What was time? Could it move backwards? Before the universe existed, where was God? If God was eternal and universal, how could He fill an eternity and a universe which didn't yet exist?

Case learned to put aside these questions most of the time, although they ambushed him at random moments, usually late at night when he couldn't sleep. Then, in the 1980s, he discovered Hawking.

He bought *A Brief History*, reading it slowly, page by page, sometimes line by line. Fascinated, obsessed, he tried to make sense of it. The arc of space-time, the notion of space and time as a continuum. The notion of a fledgling universe, infinitely small and dense and hot. Black holes: their formation, and the fate of particles drawn into them, and how time ends within them. The concept of imaginary time. Part of it he understood, part of it he had an inkling of, and part of it remained as incomprehensible to him as Sanskrit.

Two years later, he read it again, this time understanding more of it. He planned to keep at it, to read it every several years. He would never understand all of it, which didn't deter him in the slightest. He didn't understand the *Mona Lisa* either.

Aside from his work, Case was intrigued by the man himself. Stephen Hawking, frozen in the wreckage of his body, barely able to move a finger but whose mind took him to the farthest reaches of the cosmos and into the center of its black holes. Who tried to ascertain what happened in the first billion billionth of a second after the Big Bang. Stephen Hawking, who sought nothing less than the reason why we, and the universe, existed. *If we find the answer*, his book ended, *it would be the ultimate triumph of human reason—for then we would know the mind of God.*

"I'll bring it to you," Case told him.

"I'll believe it when I see it."

That night he went to Barnes & Noble and picked up *A Brief History*. He also began rereading his own copy.

On his next trip to Death Row he gave the book to Higgins, who raised his eyebrows in surprise. "I have to say, Case, I really didn't think you'd do it."

"Ask, and you shall receive."

"Yeah, that's been my experience in life."

Higgins scrutinized the cover of the book. On the cover was a photograph of a frail bespectacled man set against the background of a starry night. "That's him?"

Case nodded.

"Funny lookin' dude. What's wrong with him?"

"He's got amyotrophic lateral sclerosis . . . Lou Gehrig's disease. It causes progressive paralysis. Eventually you can't move your arms or legs, can't even speak. It's incurable."

"Kinda like when they give lethal injections. Before they kill you, they give you somethin' that freezes your muscles so you don't have spasms when you're dyin', because it spooks the witnesses."

Higgins flipped through the pages, stopping to look over things which caught his eye, scarcely mindful of Case's presence. "He got a chapter here about black holes. I read about 'em. That's when stars collapse. Gravity's so strong, they don't even give off light. Man, that's something." He put the book down. "I wonder what it's like inside one."

"Not much fun, according to Hawking. The gravitational pull would stretch you out like a piece of spaghetti. Not only that, time would come to an end."

"So you'd be trapped in there forever."

"Well, that's not altogether certain. Sometimes black holes explode with the force of millions of hydrogen bombs. And theoretically, something trapped in a black hole could be tossed out of it and reappear in another part of the universe."

"How'd he figure all that out?"

"Some people think he's the smartest man in the world."

*   *   *

"I finished it," announced Higgins, a touch of pride in his voice, when Case met with him three months hence. "That Hawking book." Their sixth meeting had just gotten underway.

"Good for you."

"Now I ain't sayin' I understand all of it. Shee-it, every page he throws some kind of curve ball at you. More I read, the more questions I got."

"For instance?"

Higgins considered. "Okay, he writes about the Big Bang, and how the universe expands outward. If that's true, then there should be a big hole in the middle of the universe, right? But he also says the universe is pretty uniform. How come? Now here's somethin' else. Nothin' can be faster than the speed of light. But Hawking says the laws of physics break down right after the Big Bang, and maybe the laws were completely different before it. So, if all the laws were different then, does that mean maybe something *could* travel even faster than the speed of light?"

"I don't know," acknowledged Case, who'd wondered about the same things.

"You know what I like the most about this stuff? It gets me outta my cell. I read about what happened billions of years ago and billions of light years away, and it doesn't matter if they got me locked up. I'm escapin', and they don't even know it."

"Ever hear of a poet named John Milton?"

Higgins shook his head.

"In one of his works he wrote, 'The mind is its own place, and of itself can make a heaven of hell, a hell of heaven.'"

"I wouldn't know about that. Never gave much thought to heaven and hell and all that crap."

"What do you think happens when we die?"

"No idea. Guess I'll find out soon enough if the fuckin' crackers have their way." Higgins's tone remained the same—calm, with an anger never far below the surface—but he began to tap one foot against the concrete floor.

"You're not curious?"

"Not particularly." Higgins looked at him dispassionately. "You don't understand that. You think a man with a death sentence hangin' over him should give it some thought."

"It's not that you *should*. But most of us do."

He paused. The tempo of his tapping quickened but he gave no other indication of heightened anxiety. "So, what's your prediction, Case? They gonna kill me?" It was the first time he'd ever asked Case this.

Case took his time before answering. "I don't know," he said finally, "but my guess would be no. The people in this state like the idea of capital punishment more than the fact of it."

"You think they should, though, right?"

"I didn't say that."

"You don't have to. You *communicate* it."

"The truth is, I'm not sure how I feel about the death penalty."

Higgins looked directly into his eyes, without his usual glare. "How do you feel about *me*, Case?"

He blushed. "My personal feelings aren't important—"

"Shee-it! Can't you give me a straight answer, just for once?"

"You don't allow me to know you very well, so I don't have a lot of strong feelings about you," he lied. A more truthful answer might have gone like this: *I dislike and fear you. You may be one of a very small number of genuinely evil people whom I've known. Not mean or immoral or amoral, but genuinely evil. When you enter the room, I could swear the temperature drops five degrees.*

He continued, "You've got a wall around you that's ten feet thick . . ."

"And that's how it's gonna stay, Case. That's just how it's gonna stay."

They talked for another fifteen minutes, mainly

about Hawking. "By the way," said Higgins as Case prepared to leave, "Ottway wants to see you."

Brian Ottway sat across from him, his eyes fixed on the floor as he rubbed his reddened, vein-lined nose. While less of a physical presence than Higgins, he was still a formidable man, six feet and about 220.

"I'll be brief," he began. "I have no interest in mental health issues, but I'd like to meet with you. Higgins lent me that book you gave him. I'd like to talk to you about it."

The next month Ottway came in with a sheet of paper. "I have questions."

"Go ahead."

He consulted the sheet. "Okay. Do you understand this stuff about antiparticles?"

Case fidgeted. "Not really. He says that every type of particle has its corresponding antiparticle—"

"Yeah, I know," Ottway cut him off. "But how did they come up with that notion in the first place? What kind of experiments did they base it on? And if pairs of particles and antiparticles annihilate each other, why is there matter at all?"

"The idea of antiparticles came from nuclear physicists." Case was in over his head. "I think Hawking says somewhere that there are many more quarks than anti-quarks. If quarks are the ultimate building blocks, that would explain why matter can accumulate. But I don't think—"

"All right, here's another one. In one of the chapters on black holes, Hawking writes about wormholes. Theoretically, if you fall in a black hole, you might come out of some fuckin' wormhole on the other side of the universe. Now what the hell does that mean?"

"I've read the book three times," admitted Case, "and I still don't know."

Case spent another twenty minutes with him, in the course of which Ottway asked about black holes, singularities, event horizons and the string theory. By their meeting's end, beads of sweat lined Case's forehead.

"We should start a club," said Ottway as he left. "The Stephen Hawking Death Row Fan Club. Arnott could join. He's no genius but he's smart enough to get some of it. We'd have to skip Marrero, though. Apart from the fact that he can't read, he still thinks the world is flat."

Case switched the order of his Death Row visits. He started with Marrero and Arnott. Then came The

Seminars, as he began to think of them. Stymied by most of Higgins's and Ottway's questions, he read other books on cosmology. He also waded through popularized works on quantum mechanics and particle physics, the most challenging books he'd ever tried to get through. His comprehension was inconsistent. While he gleaned a rudimentary understanding of Heisenberg's Uncertainty Principle, he couldn't process the concept of the Schrödinger atom, a three-dimensional bundle of vibrations instead of a miniature solar system.

Higgins still talked about himself, his case and his appeals. Ottway, true to his intentions, talked only about theories of the universe. He ignored Case's attempts to throw in a personal question or comment.

"You're doing great work with those boys," said Valentine. Despite the doctor's penchant for sarcasm, evident since the day they met, Case thought he might have meant it.

*　　*　　*

"I won't be meeting with you much longer," said Ottway as one of their meetings ended. Case had been coming to Death Row for eight months now.

"Oh?"

"It hasn't hit the papers yet, but they're giving me a date. May twenty-ninth. Unless the goddamn do-gooders pull some new rabbit out of a hat, that'll be it."

Case was too stunned to say anything. "That isn't far away," he finally offered. It was now March sixteenth.

"No, it's not." Ottway smiled when he said this. The first time he'd done so in Case's presence.

"You're certain that you want to die?"

"Absolutely." He paused and scratched his chin. "Listen, Case. I don't know much about you, and I don't want to know, but I assume you have some kind of life out there. A wife or girlfriend, or a boyfriend . . . children, a dog or cat, whatever. I assume you take vacations and long weekends. I assume there's something you enjoy. Bowling, square dancing, stamp collecting . . . something. Now if any of that's true, your life and mine have nothing in common. You may work here, but you have no idea what it's like to live here. You can't."

"Maybe not. But I do know you've still got a mind. You like playing with ideas. Why else would you bother with Hawking?"

"So what? I want to die, but that doesn't mean I

want my mind to rot beforehand. Reading Hawking makes me think. It also fills the time."

"People can use their minds in prison. They can read, they can write, they can teach other inmates—"

"Leave it alone, Case." Ottway rose and left.

Later that week, Ottway's date made front-page news throughout the state.

The Department of Corrections sent officials to Delaware and Virginia to study their lethal injection protocols. They recruited COs for the strap-down team. Although the state had switched from electrocution to lethal injection, no one had made provision for where injections would occur, and the site of the old electric chair was deemed unsuitable. Eventually they requisitioned a basement storage room as the death chamber. An adjacent room would be for witnesses, with one wall modified to include a picture window with Venetian blinds.

Editorial writers and TV commentators tossed around the pros and cons of killing him. The case, among the biggest events to hit the state in a decade, was the fodder of sermons and discussions in classrooms and bars. And the days went by inexorably, and March turned into April, and April into May, and suddenly it was time to do away with him.

By May twenty-ninth, citizens who couldn't name the governor could tell you who Brian Ottway was. The media turned his life into a scavenger hunt as they ferreted out details of his boyhood, his college days, his marriage. They badgered neighbors, distant cousins, even his father's fellow Greyhound drivers. His selections for a last meal (pepperoni pizza, butterscotch sundae) became common knowledge.

In the eye of the hurricane, Ottway himself remained casual and calm. He met with Case in a make-shift visiting room adjacent to the death cell.

Ottway strode to the table, parking his large frame in a plastic chair. "So. Looks like this is it."

Case nodded.

"Listen, Case"—he spoke without the customary brusqueness—"I know I was pretty rough on you at first. I hope you didn't take it personally."

"I didn't."

"Thing is, I appreciate what you've done for me. The talks we've had, the books you've brought, they're just about the only things I gave a rat's ass about."

"I'm glad they helped."

"I never cared too much about science. I read constantly when I ran the bookstore, but most of what I read was fiction. My wife was good at science, though.

She wanted to become a geologist, but she married me instead. Bad choice." He'd never mentioned her before.

Case waited for him to say more about her, but instead he resumed talking about Hawking. "Black holes . . . I keep thinking about them, I can't let go of it. You know how he writes about the edge of a black hole, an event horizon? I feel like I'm on the edge of a black hole, hovering there, not quite sucked in but unable to move away. Do you begin to see why I want to die now?"

"Are you frightened?" Case asked after a long pause.

"Oh, kind of. Wouldn't be human if I wasn't. And I'm human, Case. Don't much want to be, but I guess I am." He scratched an ear. "Whatever happens afterward, I think it's apt to be benign, but I'll admit that one thing scares me shitless. What if there really is a hell, and it consists of a black hole? Think of it. Spending eternity in a place where there's no light and no time, as part of an infinite density." He shuddered.

Case reached out and touched his shoulder, as lightly as he'd ever touched another human being.

"I want to go back to the cell now." He stood up abruptly and extended a hand to Case, their first and last handshake, and turned and left.

*　　*　　*

After Ottway's execution, Case did something he'd almost never done before: he took two sick days and stayed home. His stomach churned, and he had diarrhea; he felt like peeing all the time; an unrelenting headache plagued him. He was hungry but couldn't eat. Nor could he read or watch TV. Retreating to his bed, he couldn't sleep.

The next two days were the weekend. On Monday, still shaky, he returned to work.

"How are you doing?" asked Valentine.

"I've felt better."

"You've looked better."

Case glanced outside. It was early June, a bright cool morning. "I never thought they'd do it to him," he said finally. "To Higgins, conceivably, but not to him. Not even these last few weeks, when they've been getting ready for it as if it were the Mardi Gras."

"So now they've done it—" Valentine spoke in his therapist's voice. Neutral, flat, inviting elaboration.

"So now they've done it, and I can't think about anything else. Strange, because I never felt close to him. He wouldn't allow it."

"Perhaps he felt closer to you than he could say."

They fell silent, and Case looked outside again. He felt a sudden stab of claustrophobia, dagger-sharp; he'd have given anything to be walking on grass, amidst trees, unenclosed.

"You realize there'll be more of them," said Valentine, his tone subdued. "Higgins will be next, probably within a year. The racial symmetry works out. A white man first, to prove they're color-blind, and then a black one."

Later that day, when Case went to Death Row, the three surviving inmates would talk only about Brian Ottway. Even Samuel Marrero forsook his monosyllables and threw in a comment or question. *What had it been like for him? Did he walk by himself to the gurney or did the COs have to support him? Or, worse, drag him? What's the last thing he said?* (Nothing. He'd waived his final statement.) *As best as the witnesses could tell, how much had he suffered?*

They wanted to talk of Ottway, their Death Row compatriot, a founding father of their tiny, hated family. Like it or not he'd been one of them, and he was dead now (largely by his own design, since he had at least another year's worth of appeals left). The state had shown the will to kill him, and the state would try to kill the rest of them, and this was no longer an abstraction. Last week Brian Ottway had lived among them—eating and sleeping, brushing his teeth, reading, playing chess with Higgins—and he was dead now.

Arnott said he never thought it would really happen. Marrero said it was too bad. Higgins—who didn't call him a white trash piece of shit, for once—said he'd miss their chess games, and their conversations about Hawking. At least the man had half a brain.

*   *   *

"I was readin' about Schrödinger's cat," announced Higgins as he and Case sat together three months later. "Now *there* is one weird concept. Hawking writes about it in one of his essays. You know who Schrödinger was, right? Well, he imagines a cat in a box. Suppose you got a gun pointin' at it, and this gun's triggered by radioactive decay. There's exactly a fifty-fifty chance that the gun goes off. Common sense tells you that you'll wind up with a live cat or a dead one. But accordin' to quantum mechanics, you get both. This poor fuckin' cat gonna be in a mixture of live and dead states! Can you figure that one out?"

Case shook his head. "If the theories of quantum

mechanics are correct, an object doesn't have a single history, it has all possible histories. I know what the words mean but I don't understand them. I'm not sure anyone does, except a physicist."

"That mixture of livin' and dead states is kinda what it's like here," continued Higgins. "You ain't dead, but you ain't alive either. You're somewhere in between. I swear, Case, there are days when I'm not sure I'm still alive. I know I am, but it's hard to believe it."

Case felt a brief surge of sympathy for him. Very brief.

The next week Valentine summoned Case into his office. "They just turned down Higgins's latest appeal. I thought you should know before you read it in the papers."

A knot formed in Case's stomach. "Which means . . ."

"Which means that he's about to get a date."

They scheduled him for December twenty-eighth. For over forty years, there'd been no executions in the state, and now there'd be two in seven months.

Higgins's first reaction, which lasted two weeks, was complete withdrawal. He refused to see his parents or brother, or Case, or even his lawyers. He wouldn't leave his cell, wouldn't wash. The COs said he stayed in bed around the clock.

The week before Thanksgiving he asked for a shower and a haircut, and he began to go to rec again, an hour a day of walking around in a concrete courtyard. He resumed family visits, resumed a semi-active role in his defense and played checkers with Arnott. In early December he asked for Case.

Their first two meetings were monologues. Harangues. Higgins ranted about how the useless cracker lawyers who supposedly were fighting for him didn't really give a flying fuck about him, and how the cops had planted evidence on him, and how the press had turned his trial into a circus, and how his conviction was a foregone conclusion to anyone with the IQ of a bedbug. They should have lynched him on the spot and saved themselves a pile of money.

By their third meeting he was calmer. The monologues reverted back to dialogues. He still did most of the talking, though. Mostly he talked about his execution. "I been thinkin'," he tossed out, "I want you for one of the witnesses."

The blood drained from Case's face. "Why?"

"Why not? Admit it, you'd enjoy it. Be something different, change of pace from stayin' home and watchin' TV. Something to tell your grandchildren about."

"If you think I'd enjoy watching someone die, you're crazy."

"Maybe I'm crazy anyway. Possibility crossed my mind."

Case tilted his head to look up at him. "Why do you really want me there?"

Higgins shrugged. "People wanna see familiar faces when they're dyin'. What's so strange about that?"

*   *   *

"I think it's interestin' . . . they still don't know how the universe gonna end, or even if it's gonna end at all. All those theories, all those telescopes and computers, and they still don't know. Lot of them think it'll just go on expanding forever, but they ain't sure. Or will it reach equilibrium, or will it contract?" Higgins and Case were together in the death cell. It was the morning of the twenty-seventh.

"What's your own guess?"

"Well, I know the theory's fallin' out of favor, but I'd still put money on the Big Crunch. All the matter in the universe comin' together in one hot little ball, one dot, too small to imagine. Sure would be a hell of a spectacle."

"That it would be."

He stood up, began to pace. "Think about it, Case. All the atoms that ever was, every bug and every star, all squeezed into a single dot. No more life or death, no more good or bad, no more nothin', just that dot. And then, who knows, maybe the whole thing starts all over again."

Case glanced at his watch—11:20. They'd be together until noon. Then Higgins would spend the rest of the day with his mother and brother. The execution was set for a minute past midnight.

Higgins seemed to need to talk. About his family, Hawking, the chance of a reprieve, his boyhood exploits in football and basketball, about anything. His speech jumped from subject to subject like a manic frog jumping from rock to rock along a riverbank. "So," he went on, returning to the topic of the end of the universe, "if we all wind up part of the Big Crunch, that means that everything and everybody gonna be part of everything else. You're gonna be part of everyone who died before you, along with everyone alive now and everyone who ain't even born yet. Jesus and Hitler and Hawking and everyone else."

"It could be. Maybe we'll find out in twenty billion years or so."

Another manic jump. "You know what I thought about last night? That Newman woman." He hadn't referred to her by name before. Until now, she'd been *that white slut they say I killed.*

"Go on."

"Supposin' we meet after I'm dead. Be quite an encounter."

Case nodded. "What do you think you'd tell each other?" *Maybe this is it. Maybe he'll finally say he's sorry.*

"Wouldn't have to tell each other anything. We'd look each other in the eye, and everything would be clear to both of us." Case, still hoping for a flicker of remorse, still wanting to think more highly of him than he did, felt a sting of disappointment.

Noon came, and Higgins dismissed him. "I'll see you tonight. Unless they give me a reprieve, in which case I'll see you tomorrow. I think they might; I'm feelin' lucky."

Case did better than he did when Brian Ottway died; he only took the next day off. The morning after that, as he walked past Valentine's open door, the doctor waved him in.

"What was it like?" Valentine asked him.

"Like . . . it was like theater. Death as theater,

all nicely scripted. Everyone had his role. He did, the witnesses did, the COs, the Warden. You know how a play is real, but at the same time it's not? Well, that's how it was."

Case looked outside. It had snowed, and no one was there to spoil the rec yard's pristine beauty. Rumors flew that black inmates might riot following the death of Higgins, so the Warden had put the whole prison on lock-down.

"I don't think anyone wanted to go through with it, except for Newman's family, and I'm not even sure that they did." Case went on. "Not even the COs who'd volunteered for the strap-down team. It had nothing to do with guilt or innocence, or whether or not he deserved it. When the chips were down, nobody wanted to be part of it."

"What was Higgins like?"

"Beyond angry . . . the embodiment of rage. Also disbelieving. I doubt he thought they'd do it, not until they put the needle in his arm. Maybe not even then."

Case paused to sip lukewarm coffee. "So they ran the stuff into him, and his face turned peaceful—waxy. And then he stopped breathing, and he died. This is crazy, but I kept waiting for him to open his eyes. And then the play was over and the audience went home."

"Will you miss him?"

"I don't know. Maybe. God knows why." Case was suddenly sick of Higgins. At the same time he needed to go on about him. "Thelmore Higgins was a vicious, unrepentant thug. It's possible . . . no, likely . . . that the world is better off without him. But will I miss him?" He shrugged without answering.

He finished the coffee and set down the Styrofoam cup on Valentine's desk. "I think it's time for me to quit."

Valentine's head jerked up. For once he looked solicitous. "Look, Case, it's understandable you'd feel that way. You've been through two executions since the spring, you witnessed one of them. You need some time off. I can't remember the last time you took a vacation. Take one now, a long one. Go to Mexico or Aruba or somewhere, lie on a beach and drink daiquiris. When you come back, I'll give Death Row to someone else."

"It's not just that." Case's voice was less tentative than usual; for once he didn't fidget. "I've been here too long. I don't like what this place is doing to me. I don't sleep well, I don't enjoy much. Small things are getting to me, not to mention big ones. I'm tired of going through checkpoints and metal detectors to get to my office. I'm tired of looking outside and seeing barbed wire. I'm tired of feeling like a prisoner myself."

"You've been thinking about this for awhile?"

Case nodded.

"What would you do?"

"I'm not sure. Maybe buy a Baskin-Robbins franchise . . . maybe sign up for some basic science courses and take another shot at medical school. I don't care, as long as the clientele's not locked up."

"Speaking of your clientele, they'll miss you."

"They'll live." He took a few seconds to correct himself. "With the possible exceptions of Arnott and Marrero."

"Don't you think you owe it to yourself to hold off till you've had time to clear your head? Look, I've got a load of frequent flyer miles, more than enough for a round trip to the Caribbean. They're yours if you want them." No intentional grammatical errors, Case noticed.

"That's very generous of you, but I'd rather pay for it myself." He spoke slowly. "Maybe I could use a week or two off. Someplace warm, someplace where there's not a lot to do. I could hold off on a decision till I'm back." Valentine suppressed a show of relief.

"Did you ever read *A Brief History of Time*?" Case asked him.

Valentine shook his head. "Too heavy. Besides, I always figured there were things we couldn't know, things we weren't meant to know."

"The beginning and the end of time, the beginning and the end of the universe—you don't think about all that?"

"Yeah, but I don't fret about it. With high cholesterol and two daughters in college and a father in a nursing home, I figure I've got enough to fret about."

"It's had more of an impact on me than any single book I've read. There's something about it that's"—he sought the right word—"*freeing*. I remember something Higgins said about it once. He said it got him out of his cell." Case's thoughts drifted to their final conversation, when Higgins reflected on the Big Crunch. Every bug and every star, Jesus and Hitler and Hawking himself, everything and everyone, together as an infinitesimal density, beyond time and space, beyond good and evil, beyond life and death.

"He said it got him out of his cell," repeated Case. "I know what he meant. It certainly got me out of mine."

Case looked outside again, drinking in the muffled silence of a winter day, drinking in the beauty of the pristine snowfall.

THE VICTIM'S
FATHER

MARTIN DOYLE FELT ONLY A TRACE OF UNEASINESS when his son-in-law called him the first time. It was 8:30 in the evening, an hour after Sheila, Martin's daughter, had left the house to rent a movie. The drive to the video place took only twenty minutes, so where was she? Trevor Newman, her husband, wondered if she'd stopped to see her parents. He sounded fretful, but Martin thought little of it. Trevor often sounded fretful. Martin liked him, to a point, but the man could be something of a ninny. The sort who wouldn't fish with live bait because he didn't like putting a hook through a worm or minnow.

Maybe she stopped at Barnes & Noble, suggested Martin, *to pick up something for her book group. Or maybe she went to CVS or the Stop-and-Shop.* She could have gone to any of a dozen places, a hundred. *Relax,* he advised his son-in-law. Sheila would be home any minute.

At 10:30, Trevor phoned again. Still no sign of Sheila, no word from her. He'd called several friends and Sheila's two brothers. Nothing. He'd called the video place, and yes, a Sheila Newman had rented a movie three hours earlier. He'd called the police to ask about an auto accident. None involving a Sheila Newman. Trevor's voice was that of a man trying to fend off panic.

Martin no longer offered reassurances. *Let us know when you find out anything,* he directed. His mind flipped through possibilities. She could have gone to her office at Swain and Cody, to catch up on the work she never finished. Sheila, a paralegal, suffered from undue conscientiousness, or so her father felt. Her shyster bosses overworked and underpaid her, riding roughshod over her compliant nature. But Sheila would have called her husband if she'd decided to put in extra hours. Or maybe she and Trevor had had a fight, and Trevor was too embarrassed to mention it, and she left in a huff to cool off. Unlikely. Sheila and Trevor didn't fight much; he was pretty sure of that. And Sheila had never been huffy, even as an adolescent. She'd slammed no doors, engaged in no yelling matches. He considered her too soft-spoken, if anything. The soft-spoken were too easily taken advantage of. Or she could have run away. Preposterous. Unless she put on the world's best act, Sheila loved her life. She got along with her husband, seemed to, and adored Michelle, their four-year-old daughter. She took pride in their new home, a spacious Tudor. She was close to her brothers and parents, her mother in particular. She had a pack of friends.

There had to be other possibilities, if only he could think of them.

Kaye, Martin's wife, had been watching TV in the bedroom. Most likely she'd dozed off. Should he tell her? If he did, she'd have hysterics. And what could she do about it anyway? No, he would deal with this alone. Waiting . . .

He wondered, should Trevor call the cops again? They'd counsel patience and utter platitudes about how these cases almost always turned out fine. Finally he went upstairs and prepared for bed, knowing sleep would elude him. Undressing quietly, he slipped beside an already snoring Kaye.

When the doorbell rang at 1:30, he threw a bath-robe over his pajamas, his hands too unsteady to tie a knot. He *knew*, even before he opened the door and saw the cop and Trevor standing there. The cop did most of the talking. Sheila had been abducted, raped, shot and left to die in a stretch of farmland on the city's outskirts.

Martin felt as if his blood had been drained and replaced with something else, something that belonged in the veins of bats or sharks but not humans.

He remembered only fragments of the next two weeks. Trying to console Michelle. Picking out photos of Sheila for the funeral home. Picking out a casket with Kaye and Trevor. Of the funeral itself, he recalled next to nothing, except that a lot of people came. Two hundred? Three? A host of relatives. Kaye and Martin had five siblings between them and Trevor's parents had four; too many cousins to keep track of. There were lawyers and paralegals from Sheila's firm, and friends and neighbors, and fellow parishioners at Saint Augustine's Church. Members of Sheila's book group. Martin recalled that a recent selection, Capote's *In Cold Blood*, had prompted a spirited family discussion of capital punishment. Sheila, unlike her parents, had opposed it.

He remembered others who attended. The pediatrician who'd cared for her brothers and her, long retired, his black hair and Clark Gable mustache snowy white now. It must be strange, he thought, for a doctor to outlive a patient whom he'd treated since infancy.

Stan Sadlak, Trevor's co-founder and partner at the Newman-Sadlak Insurance Agency, and Stan's wife Claire. Friends since high school, Claire and Sheila had been tennis partners, confidantes and minders of each other's children.

Of her burial he remembered only that it rained. But he did recall what happened at home when the last guests left, and the last condolences offered. He and Kaye were finally alone. They went upstairs, undressed and left their clothes heaped on the bedroom floor. In bed, to their astonishment, they took solace in each other's bodies with abandon, more appropriate for teenagers than grieving grandparents. As a rule their sex life consisted of brief interludes every ten days or two weeks or so, affectionate but hardly passionate, largely silent. This time there were moans and sobs, violent thrusts and skin-rending scratches. At one point Martin thought how lucky he'd be if he had a fatal heart attack. A selfish thought—surely Kaye was traumatized enough without her husband dying during sex. Still, he had a hard time letting go of it.

He also recalled a visit from Detective Errol Steiger of the Major Crimes Unit, two days after Sheila's burial. He and the detective sat in the living room; Kaye wouldn't join them.

"We made an arrest," said Steiger.

"Who?"

"Name's Thelmore Higgins." Steiger spoke in the clipped manner of a stereotypic TV cop. "He's twenty-five. Multiple priors, including two sexual assaults. In prison more than he's been out. One very bad dude."

"Has he confessed?"

"No, but his story's full of holes. Changed his alibi three times already. None of them hold up."

Martin nodded again. "How certain are you?"

"As certain as we can be without a witness or confession."

"Why Sheila? I mean, did he know her?"

"There's no connection we know of." His speech softened. "She was simply in the wrong place at the wrong time, Mr. Doyle."

"I want him dead," said Martin, without obvious emotion. The state had a death penalty on the books, unused for a generation.

The detective gave an abbreviated nod. "It's a hope that many of us share."

In the weeks and months that followed, Martin acquired significant if disjointed information about the accused. Thelmore Higgins had no memories of living with both parents; his father left when he was three months old and no one heard from him again. His mother did three prison terms for possession and dealing before she gave up drugs for good in her thirties. Thelmore's maternal grandparents, a storefront preacher and a nurses' aide, took care of the children during her incarcerations. Despite the Reverend's stringent discipline—he favored beating Thelmore with a flashlight—the boy proved intransigent.

Sports provided a partial outlet for his energy and anger. He lifted weights and wrestled; in high school he was a second team all-state running back. There were other islands of accomplishment. A charcoal rendering of his German shepherd appeared in a grade school art exhibit. A high school chemistry project won a prize at a science fair.

He'd been in trouble with the law since the age of eleven, but details of his offenses remained unknown because they kept his juvenile records sealed. Between his times in prison, he ran a semi-successful landscaping business. He also worked as a bodyguard. At six foot three and 230 pounds he did well at this, since people rarely bothered those he guarded. He'd fathered two children, currently living in two distant states with two different mothers. Like his own father, he'd dropped out of their lives completely.

The family had its share of success stories. An aunt in California headed human resources at a Sacramento bank. An uncle, a career navy man, served on nuclear submarines; a cousin did data processing for the University of Maryland. Martin's verdict: *he didn't have to be what he became. Look at the others.*

Amassing less important facts, Martin learned that Higgins played a competent jazz trumpet and owned a full shelf of Miles Davis CDs. He had a penchant for fast cars, one of which had led to his arrest. Someone had spotted his orange Mustang parked a block away from the video place. He'd left it there before driving off with Sheila in her Mitsubishi, a gun to her head.

Martin learned that Higgins played chess, spent a month-long vacation in Trinidad each year, and had a serious allergy to bee stings. Once he almost died of one. The bee sting episode caught Martin's interest. He mentioned it in his increasingly frequent talks with Father Paul Tiernan, the priest at St. Augustine's. "I can't put it together, Father. God saves his life . . . for what? So he can rape and kill my daughter? I can't make sense of it."

Paul Tiernan, a man of fifty with dark blue eyes and

a twice-broken nose—in college he'd played hockey with less skill than ardor—peered at him over half-glasses. "I wish I had a proper answer for you, Martin. The best one I can give, the only one, isn't likely to give you great comfort. It comes down to a matter of faith, of accepting what happens as part of God's plan, which we ultimately have no way of understanding."

"Does that answer satisfy *you?*" asked Martin, not so much challenging as curious.

"Sometimes . . . not always. The collar doesn't grant a doubt-free life, you know."

"As a matter of fact, I didn't. When I was growing up, going to parochial schools and such, priests and nuns seemed absolutely sure of their beliefs."

"Perhaps they put on a bit of an act. Priests and nuns, in my experience, are altogether human, as recent painful revelations have made clear." They fell silent, drinking coffee at the kitchen table in the rectory.

"I can't shake the notion that this is my fault," resumed Martin. "I've been a salad bar Catholic, taking what I've wanted and leaving the rest. My religious life is full of contradictions. I oppose abortion, but Kaye and I used birth control for years. Sometimes I went to Mass and sometimes not. I've been known to leave things out of my confessions. I believe in God and the divinity of Jesus, but I haven't lived a Christ-like life—"

"Stop it, Martin," Father Tiernan cut him off sharply. "If you don't listen to anything else I say, listen to this and remember it: what happened to Sheila was not because you used birth control and liked to sleep in on Sundays."

"How can you be so sure of that?"

Making no answer, Father Tiernan stood up, walked over to Martin's side of the table and rested a hand on his elbow.

By the first anniversary of her death, Martin's life bore scant resemblance to what it had been. Disinclined to play golf and especially unwilling to socialize before and after games, he now took solitary walks regardless of the weather, some of them lasting hours. Formerly possessed of a hearty appetite, he had to force himself to eat—a former devotee of fast food, he could barely finish a Big Mac. Always a sound sleeper, he began to toss and turn most nights. At family gatherings his gregariousness gave way to awkward silences; he found excuses to leave early. Notwithstanding the grief-driven lust of the night of Sheila's funeral, his and Kaye's sex life dropped to nil.

There were other differences. Every Sunday, unfailingly, he went to Mass, and during the week he went as well. Never much for books, he now had two or three of them going at a time. He read about death and dying, a couple of things written by some Swiss woman doctor. He read about the death penalty, works by lawyers and theologians and even condemned criminals themselves. He read a book by a nun in Louisiana who counseled and befriended death row inmates. She was nice enough, as best he could tell from her writing, but too forgiving for his liking. Those who killed should die themselves. For Martin Doyle this didn't lend itself to much debate.

Higgins was always in his thoughts. Always, even more than Sheila. Martin thought of him as soon as he awoke and as he tried to fall asleep at night. "It's a little like being in love," he observed dryly to Father Tiernan.

In one respect, at least, his life resembled what it was before. He still worked prodigious hours. Through the years he'd built a thriving business as a plumbing contractor. If anything he worked more than ever, leaving the house before seven, often not returning until eight or nine. When he didn't work, time passed with a clammy heaviness. It was like wearing an overcoat in the heat of summer.

*   *   *

Two years passed between Sheila's murder and the trial of Thelmore Higgins. Martin followed it from first to last, Kaye by his side, with one or both sons accompanying them. He tried to take in every syllable of the testimony. But his mind wandered despite his efforts, especially when they droned on about the technicalities. The state's ballistics expert could have put a hummingbird to sleep. At other times, Martin had to fight to keep composed. Higgins broke Sheila's cheekbone with the butt of his revolver (for no clear reason, since she put up no resistance) before shooting her in the lower abdomen. In a flat dry tone—he sounded *bored*, for Christ's sake—the pathologist described the bullet's path, through bladder, uterus and colon, lodging near her spine. Martin already knew the details, having forced himself to read the autopsy report. Even so, he thought he might start to scream, or fall to his knees and bang his head against the floor.

Higgins remained the focus of his attention, always. Martin memorized every detail of his appearance, manner, dress and bearing. His gait, not quite a swagger, as he made his way to and from his seat. His rigid posture as he sat, impassive, while testimony swirled around him. His broad shoulders straining against a navy blazer. Gold studs in his ears, a diamond pinky ring. The well-formed face, the piercing eyes, the cappuccino complexion. A man who might have been a male model if he hadn't gotten sidetracked into rape and murder.

Sometimes he saw Higgins talking with an African-American couple, whom he took to be his mother and stepfather. Like Kaye and him, they never missed a moment of the trial. They sat stiffly, their eyes straight ahead, rarely talking to each other.

The lead defense attorney interested Martin more than the prosecutor. She struck him as the better lawyer: brighter, more articulate and focused. She had long brown hair and gray eyes that looked at Kaye and him with empathy. A pleasant smile, a welcome adjunct to the bleak proceedings. Of indeterminate age, she could have been in her late thirties or early fifties. He liked her, in spite of himself. How could a woman—*a woman!*—defend a man who did what he'd done to another woman? It was like a Jew defending a Nazi war criminal. It also intrigued him to see how she tried to create an effective defense when her client was so patently guilty. Higgins had not confessed, but the evidence against him was irrefutable. His fingerprints in Sheila's car. A ballistics match to his gun, also loaded with his finger-prints, which they found in a dumpster near his home. And this: late at night, a few hours after Sheila's murder, Higgins went to a bar where he threw down a row of rob roys and bragged to the guy next to him about how he'd taught some white slut a thing or two.

There was no DNA match from semen, though. He'd had the foresight to use a condom.

The jury took a full day before finding him guilty. In a separate penalty phase, it took two more days before sentencing him to die in the electric chair.

*   *   *

"I don't care what the Pope says, or the bishops." Martin paced as Father Tiernan sat at the kitchen table. "The jury did the right thing, and I'm glad. I hope I live long enough to see it happen, which I probably won't. Those appeals go on forever."

He waited for a rebuttal, but none came. He looked directly at the priest. "I suppose you think it makes me evil and vindictive to feel like that."

"Not at all. It makes you human."

Martin seemed not to hear him. "It isn't even that I hate him, although of course I do. I believe that if the acts a man commits are bad enough, he forfeits the right to life. Remember Ted Bundy? What Higgins did to my daughter, Bundy did to half a dozen women. Maybe more, I forget the body count. Why should such a creature be allowed to go on living?"

"I can give you the standard reasons. Because the death penalty has been used almost exclusively against the poor and disadvantaged. Because it leaves no way of rectifying error. Because it reduces us to the level of those we punish—"

"No disrespect intended, Father, but that's hogwash! If Higgins has any regard at all for human life, he hides it . . . and, this may surprise you, I looked for evidence to that effect. Killing Sheila meant no more to him than swatting a fly. Now killing *him*, after he's had his day in court and received the benefit of every doubt, and *then* after ten or fifteen years of appeals . . . that's completely different!"

"I'm not so sure. What Higgins did was cold-blooded, but so is an execution, despite the layers we put between ourselves and it, the judge and jury and prison guards and so on. But that isn't the main reason why many of us in the Church oppose it. This may strike you as simplistic but it's true: we don't regard it as a Christian undertaking."

Martin stopped pacing, sat opposite the priest and distractedly sipped coffee. "You may be right. You probably are. I know better than to argue doctrine with you. But I can't help it, I want him dead with every fiber of my being."

Father Tiernan paused. Then, very softly: "I worry that your hatred of him will consume you. He's occupying too much space inside your head."

"Of course he is! You think I don't already know it?"

"I didn't say that," replied Tiernan, palm raised in placation.

They fell silent. "Sorry I lashed out." Martin Doyle wasn't one to speak to a priest with impertinence. "It's just that . . . it's just . . . when someone kills a loved one, it's certain that he occupies a lot of space inside your head. Knowing that is one thing, and knowing what to do about it is something else."

Late at night in April, eight months after Higgins's trial, a full moon shone as Kaye and Martin sat in their back porch rockers. Kaye had fixed them drinks, Irish on the rocks, a splash of soda. "I need to leave you for awhile," Kaye told him, her placid tone at odds with her words.

"You're leaving—" His response was somewhere

between a question and a statement. Kaye nodded.

At first he was too stunned to speak. In thirty-two years of marriage and the two years they'd known each other beforehand, breaking up had never been an option. Not when Kaye vacillated between Martin and her former boyfriend, a stubborn sort who pursued her until a month before the wedding. Not when they struggled as newlyweds to pay bills, or after he lost $200 they couldn't spare at a casino in Atlantic City. Not even when she caught him at an office Christmas party, bestowing drunken kisses on his receptionist, an indiscretion that cost him a month of the silent treatment.

"For God's sake, why?"

"Believe it or not, this doesn't have a lot to do with you—"

"Funny, I thought it might, since we've been together for the whole of our adult lives."

"It has to do with me. Strictly speaking, more to do with Sheila."

"Sheila?" He tried to make sense of this, failing. "Sheila has been dead for close to four years now! *Sheila?*"

"Everything in this house . . . this house where the five of us lived . . . everything reminds me of her. This house, where she learned to walk and talk, played with dolls and did homework and had birthday parties." She indicated the lawn. "This yard, where she ran through the sprinkler in the summer . . ." Kaye stayed calm and dry-eyed while she spoke. Hitherto she'd been quick to cry; she could have been brought to tears by kittens and puppies in the TV pet food ads.

"Then let's sell it! We don't need the room now, we'd be comfortable in a condo half its size. We'll sell it—leave, by all means, but take me with you!"

She shook her head. "I know this isn't your fault, Martin, but every time I look at you I see her. You have the same eyes, the same round face, the same expressions." Of their three, Sheila had resembled him the most. They'd often remarked on it.

"Of course that isn't the whole story," she went on. "I don't understand all of it myself." She sipped the Irish. "I don't know if I'll survive this. Sometimes I'm not sure I want to. Not that I've considered suicide, but I often think death would be a blessing. It seems to get harder as time goes by, not easier. But if I *do* have any chance of surviving it, any chance at all, I have to go away. Alone."

Martin gulped the remainder of the drink, strode into the kitchen, returned with the Irish and refilled their glasses. "That's nonsense! Most ridiculous thing I've ever heard!" He knew he was blustering, a tack unlikely to succeed with her, but he couldn't stop. The bluster had a life of its own.

Throughout the next two hours—at times blustering, at times pleading, at times whispering—he reviewed the highs and lows of their years together, their common history. He brought up the heady first days of their courtship, their wedding on a June day in a Rhode Island chapel so close to the ocean they could smell it. Their honeymoon, five days in Florida off season, which was all they could afford. The births of children and grandchildren, and the impossible shared task of trying to come to terms with Sheila's death. The knowledge of each other's likes and dislikes, their whims and foibles, acquired piecemeal through the decades. And all the while he knew she was half-hearing him; she was somewhere he couldn't reach her.

Within a week she moved out.

*   *   *

Martin sat at Trevor Newman's dining room table, drinking iced tea and finishing a piece of cherry pie. He'd picked at the cold cuts and tortellini salad, but cherry pie was his favorite desert and he ate it with something like his old gusto. It was Father's Day, and they'd planned to have a backyard picnic, but rain forced them indoors. Sheila had been dead for seven years.

There were eight of them. Martin and Trevor. Michelle, eleven now, a beautiful child with reddish-blonde hair and startlingly light blue eyes, on the verge of womanhood. Tom and Sarah, Martin's older son and daughter-in-law, and their two sons. Mary Ellen, Trevor's girlfriend of the last nine months, a divorcee with a ready if nervous smile, the office manager for three oral surgeons. Kaye had been invited, but she was spending the day with her own father, in New Jersey. She and Martin had reached the point where they were reasonably comfortable with each other at family gatherings.

The women cleaned up, and Tom and his sons watched a Yankees game. Martin and Trevor had the dining room to themselves.

A week earlier, the governor had signed a bill changing the state's means of execution from electric chair to lethal injection. "What do you think of the new law?" asked Martin. No need to ask which one.

"I suppose it was inevitable. Do any states still use the chair? If so, there can't be more than a couple of them. What do *you* think of it?"

"I think it's overly benign," snapped Martin. "A needle in his arm and he falls asleep and it's over. Like something you'd do for a dog or cat you cared about and you didn't want for it to suffer."

"Well, from what I've read, dying in the chair can be pretty awful. Sometimes it takes five jolts to kill a man. Sometimes he'll catch on fire."

"I don't say it's preferable," said Martin irritably. "I've read about botched executions too. But lethal injections—" he shook his head—"they're *too easy.*"

Trevor finished his iced tea. "There are times, believe it or not, when I don't much care if they kill him."

"*What?*"

"Let me finish." Trevor's voice was soft but forceful. His wife's death had brought him to the brink of an abyss and, on stepping back from it, he was a different sort of man. He had more empathy for others, but he had a new firmness too. And he wasn't easily intimidated by anyone, including Martin.

"Higgins is still young—thirty-one or thirty-two, I'm guessing," he went on. "Think of him spending the rest of his life locked up in a cell barely big enough for him to do a pushup in. Another forty or fifty years, it could be. Think of him, deprived of the simplest freedoms, the freedom to stretch his legs or make a phone call or even take a shower without permission. Think of him locked up, bored beyond imagining, getting old and rotting there. Personally I find the idea attractive."

"What about Sheila? Her death deserves some retribution, doesn't it?" Martin spoke in an accusatory crackle.

Trevor gave Martin's hand the briefest pat. "Let me tell you something, Martin. I'm somewhat happy now." He pointed to the kitchen. "Mary Ellen's a great comfort to me, a great friend. And she's wonderful with Michelle, who could really use some mothering these days. We'll probably get married. But if we do, I'll still do my utmost to honor Sheila's memory. And part of that means getting on with my life. That's what she'd have wanted me to do, as I would have wanted her to do if I'd died first. We often talked about it."

"So get on with it, who's stopping you? What does Higgins's execution have to do with that?"

"If I become consumed with hating him, if waiting for his execution becomes the focal point of my existence, that isn't getting on with it. To me, it would be almost like a living death."

Martin's head jerked back as if he'd been slapped. "Is that what you think I'm doing?"

"I hope not. I don't know, Martin. I guess you're the only one who does."

The next five years of Martin's life showed a striking inconsistency. Sometimes time passed so fast it made his head spin. It seemed as if summer had scarcely come and gone and it was winter, as if Thanksgiving had scarcely come and gone and it was Easter. But sometimes time passed with a plodding inertia, and Martin felt its crawling pace as keenly as any prisoner.

In fits and starts he tried returning to the way things had been before. Missing the company of his former partners, as well as the game itself, he began to play golf again. He watched televised baseball and football games with his sons and grandsons. Twice a week he attended meetings of the Men's Club at St. Augustine's. In his business, he overcame an unwillingness to delegate. More and more he left the daily management to his son Tom, who'd worked there since his teens. He considered retiring and letting Tom take over altogether.

He often drank too much, to his consternation. Most of the men in his family—his father, uncles, brothers—fell into two groups: drunks and abstainers. Martin was among the few who trod a middle ground. He enjoyed a couple of beers or a couple of shots of Irish and let it go at that. But increasingly since Sheila's death, and especially since Kaye's departure, he drank steadily from dinnertime until he fell into a boozy stupor. Disgusted with himself, he wouldn't touch a drop for weeks, perhaps a month or two, and then the cycle started over.

There was a sprinkling of good moments. To his surprise, he enjoyed the wedding of Trevor and Mary Ellen—he almost begged off at the last minute but Michelle, in tears, had pleaded with him to attend. He let Seb, his younger son, the owner of a health and fitness club, take him to a convention in Chicago. Apart from changing planes he'd spent no time there, and he found much to like about the city. The lakefront, the Shedd Aquarium, the Museum of Science and Industry, even their weird hot dogs with celery salt and sliced cucumbers. Every two or three months he had dinner with Kaye (he also saw her at family gatherings). They didn't talk about resuming their life together, but neither did they talk about divorce.

And he kept on meeting with Father Tiernan. They met informally, usually in the rectory kitchen, inevitable coffee cups on the table. With a candor new to him, Martin told Father Tiernan of his childhood, including episodes he'd shared with no one. Fending off the sexual advances of a drunken uncle. His fury at God when his best friend died of meningitis at the age of ten. His mother's incapacitating spells of depression. He also confided, with considerable shame, his late-onset fear and dislike of black men. Martin used to think of himself as free from prejudice, but Sheila's death had changed that.

He would have regarded Father Tiernan as his closest friend except that their relations were so lopsided. The priest knew infinitely more about Martin than vice versa; Father Tiernan had always been more friendly than open. There was also a difference in status that made true friendship unlikely. Martin Doyle belonged to a generation of Irish Catholics who put priests and nuns on pedestals and kept them there, no matter what.

Twelve years after Sheila's death, the state executed an inmate named Brian Ottway. Ottway, a hulking bear of a man who looked a decade older than his age of forty-seven, had killed his wife and sons in a drunken rampage. He insisted on abandoning appeals. Legal experts said he could have kept them going for one or two more years, maybe longer, but Ottway would have none of it. He wanted to die, regretting only that the process took so long.

Following the case closely, Martin began to think that Higgins might actually be executed too. He'd never quite believed this. It seemed to him that judges went out of their way to find grounds to avoid it. But their willingness to allow the death of Ottway meant that that might be changing. Higgins, unlike Ottway, didn't want to die, but his appeals were winding down. A few experts believed he might receive a lethal injection before year's end.

*   *   *

That December, in the middle of a wind-whipped night between Christmas and New Year's, the state dispatched Thelmore Higgins with an intravenous cocktail of Seconal, pancurium bromide, and potassium chloride. Kaye sat between Martin and Trevor; Tom sat next to Martin. Seb, also eligible to be there, did not attend.

As had been the case with Sheila's funeral, Martin recalled only pieces of it. The bus that took them down a deserted road from the prison's main gate to the death chamber, away from a band of death penalty protestors who held a shivering candlelight vigil. The solemn silence of his fellow witnesses . . . Kaye's grip on his wrist as they waited (*I don't know if I can go through with this,* she muttered) . . . the warden, funereal in black suit and tie, wanting to be somewhere else . . . Higgins, still a well-formed man despite weight gained from a starchy prison diet, strapped to the gurney, not looking at them, foregoing a final statement . . . his face relaxing as the drugs seeped into him, paralyzing his facial muscles . . . the official notification of his death, five minutes and fifty-four seconds later . . . the walk back to the bus . . .

*   *   *

The man who killed Martin's daughter had been executed, moldering in a grave somewhere—no one knew its location but his family—and Martin thought he'd feel better than he did. He thought he'd fall asleep at night without Higgins staring at him in his mind's eye. January passed, and February, and he still felt no better. If anything, he drank more now, two or three beers at lunch as well as the evening shots of Irish. Periods of sobriety became fewer and farther between. He also resumed smoking, a carton of Marlboros each week. He'd given up cigarettes on his fortieth birthday and hadn't relapsed once, even when Sheila died, even when Kaye left him.

Shaving in the morning, on mornings when he cared enough to shave, he looked at himself and saw an old man staring back at him. The man had heavy-lidded eyes with deep lines etched around them and a grayish complexion. Only sixty-six, he thought he looked closer to eighty, which was more or less how he felt.

One March day, he sat in Father Tiernan's kitchen. "Tomorrow's the first day of spring," he announced with indifference. The priest nodded, waiting.

"I've always enjoyed this time of year," he went on. "The days growing longer, the world turning green again. But this year, I don't know . . ."

"You don't get any pleasure from a day like this?" The sun was shining, not a cloud in the sky, a temperature in the high fifties, a light breeze blowing.

Martin stood up, walked to a window and glanced outside. "It's nice enough."

"The weather's supposed to stay this way awhile. Any weekend plans?"

"Seb's younger daughter is coming home from college. Sunday will be her nineteenth birthday. There'll be a get-together."

"Well, that should be pleasant."

"You'd think so." The conversation sputtered.

"I was afraid this might happen," said the priest a few moments later.

"I beg your pardon?"

"I was afraid you'd expect too much from Higgins's

execution. That you'd find it anticlimactic."

Martin returned to his chair and sat down again. "I feel scooped out." He touched his midriff. "As if there's a basketball-sized hole in here. Closure, that's the word they're using now. Well, I thought I'd finally have it, whatever the hell it means, but I don't. In fact—what I mean to say—" And then, for the first time in all their meetings, he began to cry. Sheepishly, sedately, no sobbing; just a silent trickle down his cheeks. Martin Doyle was not one to cry comfortably, even in the company of a man who knew more about him than anyone in the world, who'd shepherded him through the worst days of his life. Five minutes passed before he could speak again. He pulled himself together, to a point. "*How . . .*" He asked the priest at last, "*How*, in the name of God, do I come to terms with this?"

"You'll find a way." Father Tiernan went to the sink, returning with a glass of water for him. "I can't tell you, but you'll find a way."

*   *   *

It was a hard job for Martin to get in touch with her. She had, predictably, an unlisted phone number. The reporters who'd interviewed her for the papers and

TV stations wouldn't help him, nor would the people at the prison.

In the end, Father Tiernan made it possible. The priest knew most of the city's clergymen, including those with African-American congregations. He asked around and learned that one of them, Isaiah Taylor, was well-acquainted with her. She'd been a member of his church for twenty years. Reverend Taylor said he'd pass on the request, but he doubted that she'd agree to it. Martin doubted it himself. But she surprised him. She was patient and almost civil when he called her, his speech halting. Yes, she'd meet with him, although she didn't know why he wanted to.

The choice of venue posed a problem. She didn't want him coming to her home, and he didn't want her to come to his. A restaurant or Starbuck's didn't seem right. They finally agreed to meet in the main branch of the city's public library, which had a number of small private study rooms.

So it came to pass that Martin Doyle found himself sitting opposite Brenda Rose Higgins Price, the mother of the man executed for his daughter's murder.

They met with nods, no handshake, not even a hello, avoiding each other's eyes. He looked her over, trying to be discreet about it. Taller than he remembered her from the trial, almost six feet. The same cappuccino complexion and quick disdainful eyes as Thelmore's. She had straight black hair, barely flecked with gray, and an oddly unlined face. Her age was sixty-one, but despite her drug abuse and stints in prison, not to mention her son's execution, she didn't look it.

"I still don't see why you wanna see me, Mister," she opened, more baffled than hostile. "Don't seem like we got much to talk about."

"I'm not sure either. Except that . . . we've both been through a lot. Maybe we can understand some things about each other's situation that most people can't. I don't think a person can know what it's like to lose a child unless . . ." He paused, his tongue thick inside his mouth. "There's something else. I need to find a way to forgive your son, and I thought meeting you might help me to. Not forgiving him is killing me, it's like cancer."

She glared at him. "You ever think maybe you're trying to forgive someone who didn't need no forgiveness in the first place? Someone who didn't do it?"

"No. I followed the investigation from day one, I followed every minute of the trial, and the evidence against your son was overwhelming—"

"And cops don't lie, they don't make mistakes?" Her eyes flashed. "Especially when a white girl gets killed and they think a black man did it, and any black man they can pin it on will do? You read about those thirteen men on death row out in Illinois, the ones they found were innocent? There been plenty of other cases like that too, all over the country."

"The fingerprints, the ballistics and the rest of it—you didn't find all that convincing?"

"Listen, Mister. I know my son. He wasn't never easy, even when he was a toddler. And I know I made things worse. As a mother, I did an awful job back then. I made every mistake possible, and I gotta carry the guilt for that to my grave. He done his share of bad things in life, I guess I know it better'n anyone, but he wasn't no killer. I *know* that, sure as I know you're sitting here."

Martin remembered one of his conversations with Father Tiernan. *People have an extraordinary ability to believe what they want or need to,* the priest had told him. Terrorists who killed children believed they served the greater good. Battered wives who'd been hospitalized a dozen times believed their husbands really loved them. And the mother of a killer believed in her son's innocence, despite enough evidence to convince twelve jurors, or twelve hundred. He changed the subject.

"How've you managed to get through this?" he asked her.

"With it all I been lucky. I got some real fine people in my corner. Reverend Taylor and the rest of them at church. My friends in AA and NA. My husband—him, most of all. I woulda been dead if it weren't for him. Or else I woulda used. Same thing, pretty much." She paused. "How 'bout you?"

"My sons and their families have been there for me. Trevor too . . . Sheila's husband. And there's a priest I've gotten close to."

"You didn't mention your wife."

"We're not together now," he said without elaboration.

"Too bad."

They fell silent. "I thought I could put the whole thing behind me," he said slowly, "at least begin to, after the execution. But that hasn't been the case."

"You saw it, right?"

"Yes."

"How'd you feel when it was happening?" The question was cool and clinical; she might have been his therapist.

"You really want to talk about this?"

"Wouldn't ask you if I didn't."

He formed an answer carefully. "I felt anger, followed by relief, followed by emptiness. I felt as if a great weight had been lifted from me, but another one took its place." She nodded curtly.

"How'd *you* feel when they executed him?"

"How you *think* I felt?" she hissed. "If I coulda got hold of a machine gun, I might have shot me a bunch of white men, gone crazy like some whack job in a post office. Never felt that kinda anger in my life. But then I prayed with Reverend Taylor, and he kept telling me how Thelmore was in a better place now. He stayed with us all night. And the good Lord took away my anger. Most of it."

"It's strange," said Martin, "I wanted to see him dead, but at the same time I feel bad that you lost a son. No one should lose a child."

"You sure got that one right."

"What're you gonna do now, Mister?" she asked him after another silence.

"I don't know what you mean."

"Well, I'm guessing you been waiting years for Thelmore's execution. So, it finally happened. Where you gonna go from here?"

"I don't know," he answered her, "but for starters I plan to retire. Give my business to my son. He pretty much runs it anyway. Then I want to move. Too many memories in this city."

"Moving . . . I think about that too. Where you gonna move to?"

"Once in awhile, when the kids were young, we took vacations in western Maine. It's beautiful country, full of hills and lakes and virgin forest. I want to buy a small house there, by a lake. Spend the days fishing, hiking, reading. Funny, how I hardly read at all before Sheila died, mostly a *Time* or *Sports Illustrated*. Now I read all the time."

"What kinda stuff?"

He shrugged. "It varies. The Bible, books about religion. Recently, some books about Ireland. I don't know much about my origins, but I'd like to. Not a lot of fiction, though. I've never been one for story-telling."

"Me neither. If it ain't real, don't bother me with it."

"I want to be where I don't have a great deal to do with other people," he went on. "My sons and their families, and the priest I mentioned; that's about it. And I hope to come down to see my wife once in a while, and maybe she'll come up. I'd like an isolated area, but one that's not too far from here."

He rubbed his palms together. "A place where I can meditate . . . pray . . ."

When she spoke, her voice was less abrasive than before. "They got this way of thinking in AA and NA— if you're angry with someone, you need to pray for him. You oughtta try praying for Thelmore's soul. I ain't angry with your daughter, but I'll pray for hers as well. Just to balance things out."

He considered this at length. It occurred to him: *To pray for the soul of Thelmore Higgins would be, without a doubt, the strangest thing I've ever done. The same Thelmore Higgins who did things to my Sheila that I still can't think about. The same Thelmore Higgins whom I yearned to see dead, whom I wanted to burn in hell forever.* Still, he had to admit the idea possessed a certain attractiveness. In any case, what was there to lose? Maybe . . .

"All right," he said with a slow deliberate nod. "Let's do it." They caught each other's gaze, and this time neither of them turned away.

UNACCOMPANIED MINOR

LYING HERE, SO MANY HOURS TO KILL, boredom spreading through me like the Black Death, I pass time playing games with my memory. I try to see how far back I can go with it.

There are snapshots of New Haven. Glimpses of Yale's spires and the beaches on Long Island Sound. The beach scenes are more vivid. In one of them I have an image of myself on a yellow blanket wedged between my parents. The image might come from a photo I saw, but I doubt it. The feelings are too real. I shut my eyes and can almost feel the heat of their bodies and smell their musky tanning oil.

They were still together, so it must have been before my fifth birthday. The next summer, when Dad finished his residency, they split up. He stayed in New England, eventually becoming chief of radiology at a hospital in

Rhode Island. My mother and I moved to New Mexico. She says she went because of a good job offer. He says she went to scare him into getting back together. *If you don't stay with me there'll be 3,000 miles between your son and you.* I don't know which version is the truth. Maybe neither, maybe both.

*   *   *

Some of my earliest memories are of flying.

Unaccompanied minors, they called us. Thanks to the high divorce rate, and ex-spouses who put as much distance between each other as they could, there were lots of us. Still are, I imagine.

It went like this. Mom would bring me to the check-in counter—or Dad, if I were heading back—and fill out a form. Then she'd put me on the plane. They boarded us ahead of other passengers, with women who had babies and people in wheelchairs, and I'd meet the flight attendants. For the most part everyone was very nice. I often got a tour of the cockpit before takeoff.

There were no direct flights, so I had to change planes, mainly in Atlanta or Chicago. That could be a pain, especially with tight connections. There were always air traffic delays or something. They hustled me through the corridors like a puppy on a leash, no time to get a Coke or play a video game. Sometimes there wasn't even time to pee.

I tell people about my trips as an unaccompanied minor, beginning when I was under six, and they feel sorry for me, which I hate. But I'll admit that there were times when I milked it for all it was worth. I've told girls about it, building sympathy. Poor Jeff, parents splitting up before he started kindergarten, traveling thousands of miles on his own and blah blah blah. A few times it helped me get laid.

I was never afraid of flying. At least not that I knew of, not that I'd admit. When you start so young and do so much of it, what's to be afraid of? Takeoffs and landings were gentler than the rides I liked in amusements parks, the roller coaster and tilt-a-whirl. My parents were more apprehensive, especially Mom, who never cared for flying. They put me on the plane with tight fake smiles, squeezing my hand longer than necessary. Sometimes, when they met me, I heard them sigh in relief. But even if I'd been frightened, I would have tried to keep it from them. Their own fears were bad enough. Better to hide behind my Huck Finn face—cheerful, nonchalant.

Of course there were disturbing moments. In thunderstorms over the plains and prairies, a jet felt as flimsy as a leaky boat. Once, over Texas, the pilot said we had to make an emergency landing because of the weather. I didn't understand. I had a window seat, and everything looked fine out there. But when I looked out the other side, I saw a muddy sky, and bolts of lightning flashing in the distance, and rain pouring down in thick black sheets. The pilot brought us down, almost in a nose dive. We spent two hours on a runway in Odessa.

The incident that spooked me most had nothing to do with weather, though. Once, when I was ten, I had to change planes in Chicago. A few days earlier they'd had a crash there. I could see the burnt-out hull of a jumbo jet as we made our approach. Soot stained the fuselage, the wings were crumpled, and the ground around the crash was charred. I wondered what it had been like onboard as the plane plummeted out of control. I wondered about dumb things, like how many kids had been aboard, and if the passengers were bad people whom God decided to punish. That struck me as unlikely. Surely bad people took other flights, on other airlines, but how else does a child make sense of it? Maybe God used some kind of formula, like if over half the passengers were bad, the plane went down. I think we'd been studying fractions then.

When Dad picked me up in New England, I didn't

talk about the wreckage. Of course not. "How was your trip?" he asked, as usual. "Fine," I answered him, as usual. He breathed his customary sigh of relief, and I hid behind my Huck Finn face. A boy happy to see his father. The thing is, I *was* glad to see him. Three or four months might pass between our visits, and I'd miss him.

But incidents like that were few. Flying didn't thrill me, but I didn't fear it either. Mainly I saw it as a fact of life. If I wanted to spend time with Dad, I had to do it, period.

Once we took off, the main problem was boredom. My parents did their best to alleviate it. I always had a knapsack full of coloring books (real books, as I grew older), and toys and puzzles. They helped, but the flights still took forever. Even then I used to pass the time playing games with my memory. Trying to remember the details of movies I'd seen, or who came to my fifth birthday party, or details of when my parents were still together. Anything, whatever.

*   *   *

The daydreams end when my cell door snaps open. One of the Correctional Officers, COs, stands in front of me. I'm lying on my stomach, so I can't make out his face.

"Okay, Zwerling, it's time for rec." I recognize the voice and accent. Martinez. He's one of the better COs. Which is to say, he doesn't spit in my food or coffee. He doesn't wake me with a blinding light in my eyes or a fist in my ribs. He doesn't withhold my cigarettes or showers on a whim. Sometimes I've had conversations with him for the better part of an entire minute.

"Okay." I rise from the bed unsteadily, move to the sink, splash cold water on my face. Then I put on sneakers, which takes no time at all since I have no shoelaces. Suicide precautions.

I have a single cell in the hospital wing. Piss-poor excuse for a hospital. No X-rays, no OR, no nurses fluffing our pillows. The doc comes in for an hour or two a day. On some shifts they don't even have a medic.

Not all the inmates here are sick. Like me, a lot of them are in PC, protective custody. The rest have all kinds of things wrong with them. There's an old guy here, Yurdin, who got the creepy crawlies when he came off two weeks of Night Train. Sweetnam is a black kid, built like a Big Ten varsity wrestler, with a wired jaw. They broke it when they arrested him. Some are middle-aged guys like Biggens, admitted because they said they had chest pain, which is an easy way to get here. No one wants you to have a heart attack in jail, because it makes for too much paperwork. Mueller is an eerie dude with tics and a smile that makes you want to run for cover, hasn't said a dozen words since they brought him in. He tries to look more mild-mannered than I think he really is; there's something quietly vicious about him. Reyes is a Cuban who has seizures. They think it's due to AIDS. Plenty of guys with AIDS down here, more druggies than faggots, although we do have a flaming queen who calls himself Veronica, who uses rouge and lipstick.

I leave my cell and saunter down the corridor to the CO's station. Rec means that those of us who are ambulatory, who aren't in punitive seg or in restraints, can walk around outside for half an hour. Which may not sound like much, but I do, in fact, look forward to it. One of the highlights of the day.

They open a series of steel doors and we wander out to a concrete patio, surrounded on all sides by different parts of the jail. At any given time there are more than 700 inmates here. The jail takes up an entire city block. Overhead, the sky is a hazy pale blue. It would be nice to see some grass as well, but you can't have everything.

Dillard and I nod at each other, and he comes

towards me. We walk together, in a slow clockwise circle around the patio, a few steps apart from the others. They let the hospital inmates out in groups of six. He and I are the only white guys in our group.

This is the second day they've let him out. He's doing better now, at least he makes sense when you talk to him, but he was crazy as a coot when they brought him to the hospital wing. You could hear him all night long, yelling back to his voices. *"Leave me alone, you fuckin' whores, leave me the fuck ALONE!"* They're giving him a load of medication, and he walks as if he's as old as Yurdin.

"How's it going?" I ask.

"Okay." He doesn't look okay. His face is frozen and puffy. Probably due to all his meds. You wouldn't believe he's only twenty-two.

He pauses. Lots of pauses when you talk to Dillard. "How's it goin' with you?"

"Okay." Sure I am. I've been arrested on felony charges, and I'm broke, and my nerves are shot to shit, and I'm thousands of miles from either parent, and my public defender's a burned-out cipher who got his law degree collecting box tops, who couldn't win a case defending a nun on a vice rap.

"I'm gonna have a visit after lunch. Martinez, he

said my ma's comin' up." The puffy face tries to smile, fails.

"That's nice."

"Pa can't come, he's gotta work. Pa, he works for the Highway Department." This is more than he's ever told me. He's a chatterbox today.

Another pause. "You said you're not from around here."

"I told you. I grew up in New Mexico but I spent a lot of time back East, in New England. It's where my father lives."

"New England, is that like a different country? They got different money and things there?" Dillard's body of knowledge contains large gaps. Yesterday he asked me how many months are in a year.

"No, Dillard," I explain, "New England is part of this great land of ours."

"What's your dad do?"

"He works in a hospital," I answer quickly. None of the inmates know the old man's a doctor, and that's how I want to keep it.

"I hate hospitals. Especially the funny farms, they're the worst. Been in and out of 'em since I was a kid. Must have been in 'em ten times already. Probably have to go to one again."

I give a noncommittal grunt. In fact he'll be incredibly lucky if he makes it to a mental hospital. He beat an old woman to death with a baseball bat because his voices said she was a she-devil. Good thing for him he was so crazy. There's a crowded death row in this state.

We walk some more, saying little. Dillard has already said twice as much as usual. When he does talk, he mainly bitches about the food. He says he's gonna gag if they give us hot dogs and sauerkraut again for lunch, it gives him the farts.

We're about to go back inside when he turns to me. "They said you're waiting for some tests."

"Who said?"

"That nigger medic, Washington, was tellin' someone."

"People have big mouths here."

*　　*　　*

One thing about flying the way I did, it made me learn how to talk to strangers. How to strike up conversations. It was hardest to do this with businessmen, who liked to keep themselves busy with their laptops and their spreadsheets. Women in their fifties and sixties were the easiest. As a rule they were grandmotherly types, friendly and solicitous. *Why, I've got a grandson just about your age*, they'd say. Usually they carried food with them, chocolate bars and bags of nuts, and they always shared what they had.

People often told me about themselves, and some of their stories were interesting. Once I sat next to a Mormon lady who'd done missionary work in Italy. That struck me as kind of weird. I thought missionaries only went to places like Africa. Another time, I met a Navy guy who served on a nuclear sub. I tried to imagine what that must have been like, staying miles under the water for months on end, with enough nukes to blow up half the world. I wondered if they ever went crazy down there. And if they did, what kept them from starting World War III?

Sometimes, flying back to New Mexico, if I met a man I liked and he didn't wear a wedding ring, I thought about trying to fix him up with Mom. I made up whole scenarios, how I'd introduce them while the three of us waited at the baggage carousel, and their eyes would meet. Love at first sight. There'd be a whirlwind court-ship, and a few months later they'd get married. Mom would be ecstatic. We'd live happily ever after. A real-life fairy tale. We'd live in the country with lots of land. We'd own horses. I'd have brothers and sisters.

Dad's new wife has a daughter, Pia, from her first marriage, but we aren't close. She was always a snotty little thing, two years younger than I am, with a turned-up nose and too many freckles. Pia's in college now, I don't know where and I don't care. No doubt she's majoring in making pot-holders or some other kind of summer camp horseshit.

I guess I shouldn't knock her. What the hell, at least she's in college and not in jail.

Mom didn't remarry for ten years after the divorce, didn't even date for the first three years. I never understood that. She's pretty enough and knows how to have fun when she wants to. She was very sad when they split up, which she tried to hide from me, but of course she couldn't. I used to hear her cry herself to sleep. The walls were thin and I heard everything. I must have been furious with Dad for leaving her. At least that's what my ex-shrink, Farnsworth, used to say. He said I had plenty of anger towards both of them. If so, I wasn't aware of it. At least not then.

To the extent that I thought about it (very little), I thought I'd done okay with their divorce. I wasn't haunted by a bunch of golden memories of when we were still a family, and I knew better than to want them back together (Farnsworth disagreed). As children of divorced parents go, I had it made. We weren't rich, but Mom and I lived decently. Sometimes Dad played games with alimony, but he sent the child support on time. He always stayed a part of my life, despite the distance. Three times a year he flew me to Rhode Island and once a year he came to New Mexico. When we weren't together he called me every week, without fail. Once he called me from the hospital where they were treating him for kidney stones, and once he called me from Madrid where he was at a medical meeting.

I thought I'd done okay with their divorce, but maybe Farnsworth was right. Sometimes I had dreams, or pieces of dreams, of the three of us together. Even now I still have them.

*   *   *

By the time they herd us back inside, gleaming metal food carts line the corridor. It's a few minutes before eleven.

We pick up our trays, and Dillard and I sit next to each other in the hospital mess. Dining's communal, except for those of us who are bedridden or in restraints.

Two other white guys join us. Yurdin, who's over the worst of the DTs now, and Corcoran. Of all the ones I've met in here, Corcoran has to be the most pathetic. He's a frail thin type with glasses a half inch thick, not too bright, a school janitor accused of child molesting. If you have to diddle kids, don't get arrested. Other inmates harass you, rip you off, use you as a punching bag from the minute you're locked up. The COs don't stop it. Sometimes they join in.

Corcoran's in PC now. He has three fractured ribs and a broken cheekbone. Yesterday we were in the shower together and I almost puked. He'd been kicked in the groin, and one of his balls was about the size and color of an eggplant.

I lift the cover off my plate and steel myself for what's beneath. A lot of times you can't recognize the food. They overcook everything, so all the vegetables have the consistency of applesauce. Orange glop might be squash or carrots, white glop might be potatoes or turnips, and so on. Everything's covered with gray gravy. But guessing vegetables is easy compared to meat, which is impossible, except for chicken. You can tell it by the bones. Things have really gone downhill here since the French chef died.

Today it's spaghetti with meat sauce, pinto beans, white bread with oleo and a cupcake. The spaghetti sauce doesn't look too bad, but even though I'm hungry,

I can't eat it. There's a story the inmates pass around, supposedly true, about how someone in the kitchen took a shit in it a couple of years ago. In this state, goes the joke, murderers have a choice between lethal injection and spaghetti sauce.

No one talks while we're eating, but every so often Yurdin mumbles to himself. I can't make out what he's saying. *Karr'warr, karr'warr,* it sounds like. Yurdin has his lower plate, but not his uppers, which makes him nearly impossible to understand.

"Whaja say, ole man?" asks Dillard.

Yurdin dribbles spaghetti sauce down his chin and concentrates. "Karr'warr. Karr'warr vet. Shou' be in a Vee Aye 'cause of Karr'warr."

"He says he's a Korean War Vet and he should be in a VA hospital," I translate. Yurdin nods vigorously, so vigorously that a glob of spaghetti sauce flies off his chin and lands on Corcoran's cupcake.

"Hey, watch what you're doin'! Stupid ole bastard," mutters Corcoran, who tries to be intimidating. But this is hard when you weigh 130, and your glasses are half an inch thick, and the whole left side of your face is one big scarlet bruise.

I toy with the food but mainly I glance at Yurdin, who sits across from me. "How old are you?" I ask him.

He squeezes his forehead into furrows and works his mouth while he concentrates. The way he works his mouth is hard to describe, as if he's chewing and smacking his lips at the same time. He never stops.

"Dunno—wait a minute—seveneesev. Yeah, that's it, I'm seveneesev." He's only seventy-seven. I'd have him pegged for close to ninety. You drink Thunderbird and Night Train for fifty years, and you live in welfare hotels and alleys, and it takes a toll.

I can't stop looking at him. Something about him fascinates me. His face has too many lumps and bumps and scars to count. His nose, flattened at the bridge, bends sharply to one side before it ends in a red fleshy bulb. I wonder what he looked like when he went to Korea. He would have been about my age now. I try to imagine him in uniform, all spiffed up, saying good-bye to his parents and maybe his girlfriend. Did he see a lot of combat? Is that what did it, what turned him into a wino? Did he have any plans for when he got out? Marry the girlfriend, go back to school? Once upon a time he had a *life*, presumably. I wonder how he got from there to here.

*   *   *

Yurdin has a big head start on me, but I know a bit about booze myself.

I started to drink when I was eleven. Not much, at least at first. A shot of Dad's vodka after he and my stepmother went to bed, or a glass or two of wine in the kitchen when Mom had guests for dinner. Both of them were lightweight drinkers, so they were never as suspicious as they should have been. I got away with it easily.

The first time I really got loaded was on an airplane. It happened one Christmas vacation when I flew up to see Dad. I must have been around thirteen.

The flight was from Albuquerque to Atlanta. We stopped in Dallas, and this Paul Bunyan type with a red beard and blazing blue eyes got on and flopped next to me. We were on a DC-9 with three/two seating, and he and I had two seats to ourselves.

The plane had barely left the Jetway when he pulled a bottle of Yukon Jack from the inside pocket of his leather jacket. He smiled at me and winked. "They don't like it when you drink yur own booze. They lose money, 'cause they wanna sell you theirs. Ain't nothin' like a shot of hooch. Best thing on God's earth, next to poon tang." I nodded sagely, although I wasn't sure what *poon tang* meant.

"Billy Joe Dobson's the name." He offered me a hand, twice the size of mine.

"I'm Jeff Zwerling."

The plane taxied, the flight attendant gave her spiel, and we took off. Billy Joe's patter never stopped. By the time we reached our cruising altitude I knew his Daddy worked in the Fort Worth stockyards ("good man when he's sober, which is three or four days a year"), and his Momma, God rest her soul, had died of sugar diabetes, and his sister was a dancer at the Boom Boom Club in Houston, and his poor ole brother was in the pen down in Huntsville 'cause some pussy said he'd raped her, which was bullshit, 'cause everyone knew she asked for it. Billy Joe himself worked on an oil rig.

We were only fifteen minutes out of Dallas when he killed the bottle. He pulled another from his magic leather jacket. As he screwed the top off, he turned to me and winked again. "Say, son, how about a nip yourself?"

I smiled and nodded, trying to keep my joy contained. I'd had traveling companions who were friendly enough, but never before had I sat next to Santa Claus.

To tell the truth, the rest of the trip is pretty much a blank. What I do remember is altogether pleasant. The sweet sting of Yukon Jack as it burned its way down my throat. Laughing my head off at Billy Joe's dumb jokes. Both of us having giggling fits as I tried to eat dinner and dumped salad in my lap (you still got meals on short flights then). A sense of flying, independent of the airplane—I really did feel *high*. A break from worrying about my grades which were already sliding, or my new zits, or any other big or little problems. A sense that all was well and always would be.

Billy Joe had quite an impact on me. For a few weeks, I even kicked around the notion of working on an oil rig.

Drunk though I was, I had the presence of mind to make myself throw up in a men's room in Atlanta. Then I bought a pack of gum. Dad would meet my plane, as usual, and I didn't want to blow Yukon Jack fumes in his face. I needn't have bothered. He took a look at me and asked if I'd been airsick. I nodded and gave him some nonsense about the turbulence. Dad can be such an idiot. Sometimes I wonder how the fuck he made it through medical school.

A significant consequence of this particular trip: I learned that I loved being drunk, and I resolved to stay that way as much as possible.

*　　*　　*

After lunch they give out meds, and then there's count, and then they lock us up again. We stay locked up until 2:30, the start of visiting hours. I almost look forward to going to my cell. The heavy food always makes you want to nap. Sleep is a scarce commodity in here. TV, yelling, bright lights and clanking doors make it all but impossible. Worse if you're on suicide watch. They check you every twenty minutes around the clock.

On top of all that, there's the goddamn P.A. system. Most of the COs have walkie-talkies, but the P.A. is always blaring anyway. *ALL AVAILABLE OFFICERS, CODE ORANGE, C-BLOCK WEST! MEDIC WASHINGTON TO ADMITTING STAT! NOTICE, ALL INMATES, THE LAW LIBRARY WILL BE CLOSED AN HOUR EARLY TODAY! COUNSELORS REED AND JEFFCOAT, CALL CENTER RECEPTION! ALL AVAILABLE OFFICERS, CODE ORANGE, CANCEL!*

I sprawl on my bunk, fully clothed, and doze off in a flash. The nap is shattered by Martinez banging his keys against my cell door. "Get up, Zwerling. Miz Andrews wanna see you."

Odetta Andrews is a counselor attached to the hospital wing. She's a fat black woman with the smallest eyes and biggest boobs I've ever seen, like volleyballs. Her age is hard to guess, anything from thirty to forty-five.

I've met with Odetta twice, and we decided right away we couldn't stand each other. Too bad, because your counselor's the most important person in your life in here. She gets you passes to the commissary and library, she runs interference between you and the COs, she puts you on suicide watch and takes you off (the shrink's supposed to do this, but most of the time he does what the counselor tells him). She can goose the doc or dentist into seeing you right away, or she can slip your request to the bottom of the pile. They talk about another counselor who hated this one inmate. He complained about a toothache for a month but she kept losing his requests to see a dentist. By the time he got to see one, he'd already lost two teeth. Not to mention, he'd been in pain for a month.

Counselors will do small favors that make jail more tolerable. Find you a pad of writing paper or a magazine that's not as old as you are, things like that. Sometimes they'll really go to bat for you. They'll advise your family on how to make bail, or talk to your lawyer, or even talk to the DA.

Martinez escorts me to Odetta's office, and I vow to

be polite and friendly despite of myself. To charm her. But I know it won't work. People who work in jails are charm-proof.

She waits for me in a windowless cubbyhole, squinting down at my file. There's a folding metal chair and a tiny bookcase, the only furniture besides her desk. No decorations, apart from some postcards of New York City taped to the walls. The UN, the Empire State Building, the skyline at dusk.

"Sit down, Zwerling." She motions me to the chair without looking up. When we met, I made the mistake of not waiting for an invitation. *LISTEN, BOY, YOU DON'T SIT DOWN IN THIS OFFICE UNTIL I TELL YOU TO, YOU UNDERSTAND ME NOW?*

She finally glances up at me, nods curtly. "You look better. Swelling around your eye is down, and it's not so discolored."

I touch my right eyelid, which still feels like it sticks out an inch farther than the left one. "It's not so tender anymore."

"Good." Is she in a halfway decent mood today? Maybe, just this once, we'll get along.

That's it for small talk. "Now, Zwerling, there are some questions I didn't get to last time. Were you ever in treatment or counseling?"

"Yeah, for about a year."

"How old were you?"

"Sixteen." Four years ago, another lifetime.

"Reason for therapy?" She sounds like she's firing off a checklist.

"Lousy grades. I'd just been put on academic probation."

"How much were you drinking?"

"A six-pack or two." I neglect to mention the hard stuff.

"Other drugs?"

"Anything available. Pot . . . I used a lot of it. Once in a while, cocaine. Tried LSD, but I had a real bad trip."

"Did your therapist know about the drugs and alcohol?"

"He knew I got drunk from time to time. But he was more interested in my parents' divorce and things like that. It was easy to con him."

She stops writing, folds her hands. "It's been too easy for you to con people, Jeffrey."

Jeffrey. First time she's called me by my first name, and it catches me off guard, like a slap. First time anyone has called me by my first name since the arrest.

She asks me more about Farnsworth, and about using drugs and booze, and if I'd ever thought about getting treatment for it, which would have been the last thing I wanted. Once in a while she almost sounds kind, and I wonder if I'm in the right office. But she doesn't call me *Jeffrey* again. Must have been a slip.

She looks at her watch and closes my folder, which signals that our time is over. "Okay, Zwerling. Anything else?"

"Yeah. Listen, Miz Andrews, I'm really not about to kill myself. Would you *please* have them take me off suicide watch? It's hard enough to sleep in this place."

She studies me with her tiny eyes, deciding whether to believe me. "I don't know, Zwerling. You was one real bad case when they admitted you."

I bristle. "Wouldn't you be?"

She says nothing. "Besides," I press on, "that was what, four or five days ago? I'm better now."

She clucks her tongue against the roof of her mouth. "Okay," she says finally. "But you best pay attention to me, Zwerling. Try anything and I'll put you back on it for the rest of your time here."

"I won't."

I start to stand and leave but she motions me to wait a moment. "One more thing. After we talked last time I took the liberty of calling your father—"

"Goddamn, you *promised!* I never would have

told you who he was or where he was if I knew you'd do that . . . *you promised!*" I feel the color rising in my cheeks. I want to take my chair and fling it in her fat ugly face, I want to call her every name I know. But I have to keep control, I *have* to. This cunt could make my life a living hell for looking at her cross-eyed. She could take away my mattress and have me shackled hand and foot over bare bedsprings.

Surprisingly, she tolerates my anger. When she speaks, in fact, her voice is softer. "Any parent would wanna know. I would, if a child of mine was in your boat. Besides, he might be able to help you, Jeffrey."

Jeffrey. Twice in a single meeting.

"Your charges—" she goes on, "well, it ain't like you chopped up kids or something. A good lawyer, a treatment program, and who knows? A good lawyer might make the case that you already been punished sufficiently. "

She folds her hands. "And maybe you're just a little bit relieved? Maybe you hoped I'd tell him?"

"I didn't. I knew he'd find out about this sooner or later, but I wanted to put it off as long as possible."

"Why?"

The anger dies down, and all of a sudden it's hard to speak coherently. "Because I don't want him to know how badly I fucked up—" I summon my last reserves of self-control to keep from crying. It would be the last straw, to cry in front of her. I'd never forgive myself.

*   *   *

As I grew older, careening through my teens, I continued to fly between my parents' homes but I was no longer an unaccompanied minor. At some point, I forget just when, the airlines decided I was old enough to fend for myself.

When I flew, I was always drunk or stoned. I carried my own bottles in my pockets, like Billy Joe. As he said, no sense paying those outrageous airline prices. Besides, they might balk at my fake ID. I also liked to smoke a joint or two before I left and another one in the men's room, when I changed planes in Atlanta or wherever. This was risky, since I never knew who might walk in on me, but I did it anyway.

I liked to fly in a balmy daze, I made a point of it. Even Farnsworth picked up on that. He thought I drank, at least in part, to get my parents' attention. Especially Dad's. He thought I just about begged to be discovered. But Dad, who makes a very good living scrutinizing CT-scans and MRIs, whose attention to detail is usually phenomenal, managed not to notice. Even when I passed out in a john at O'Hare and missed a connection, he *still* managed not to notice. I told him I fell asleep because I was up all night studying before the day I left, and he bought it! Do you believe that?

Not everyone was taken in.

Two years ago, I flew to New England from Texas, where I pretended to be a college student. I was spending part of my spring vacation with Dad. He planned to take me skiing in New Hampshire. I really didn't want to make the trip. Skiing has never been a great love of mine, but I played along because it's something he enjoys. Myself, I'd have preferred to spend the time partying.

So there I was, flying up reluctantly, nursing a hangover, beginning to feel the kick of whatever drugs I happened to be using then. We took off, and I pulled out a bottle of Yukon Jack. I always drink it when I fly, as a tribute to Billy Joe.

If the passenger next to me looked like someone who'd have a fit, I'd drink in the lav. But on this flight the guy looked as if he'd be cool about it. Hefty, with curly black hair and a swarthy complexion. Blue collar. Friendly way about him. Mid-thirties, I figured.

He glanced at me and smiled. "Yukon Jack . . . that

sure brings back some memories! There was a time when I put away a pint of it a day. Wash it down with a six-pack of Coors."

I smiled back. "Would you care for some?" Always nice to have a drinking buddy.

He waved me off. "Thanks, but I haven't touched the stuff for five years now. Got to be something of a problem. Two counts of drunk driving, blackouts, waking up with the shakes . . . nope, I figured enough's enough."

My spirits sank. The last thing in the world I wanted was to hear about his quitting. But I was too well mannered to ask him to please shut up about it. Besides, there was something about him that made me curious. His eyes, I think. Gray and wide-set, missing nothing.

I wanted to talk to him, but not about booze. "Are you from Texas?"

He shook his head. "I've been there three years now, but originally I'm from Rhode Island."

"Where?"

"A town called Galilee. A tiny place, a speck on a map. You probably never heard of it."

"I've been there lots of times. My father only lives half an hour away."

He threw back his head and laughed. "Well, how

about that! I didn't think *anyone* had heard of Galilee. I mean, anyone not born and bred in Rhode Island."

I debated whether to take another swig of Yukon Jack, decided not to. "Dad took me on deep-sea fishing trips from there when I came up to visit him. They were some of the happiest times I had when I was a kid. The bluefish—God, how they'd fight!"

The gray eyes lit up. "Ounce for ounce, there's more fight to a blue than anything. And they taste good too, if you cook them right. Otherwise they're awful, as though they've been dunked in castor oil."

"Dad used to soak them overnight in buttermilk." I paused and glanced again at the Yukon Jack on my lap. As much as my belly yearned for booze, I felt a reluctance to drink in front of him. "You must have done a lot of fishing growing up."

He laughed again. I liked his laugh, which was deep and convincing. "Every day! I practically lived on boats. My father's a commercial fisherman. He comes from Portugal. The family fished for generations there."

"Are you a fisherman yourself?" He looked the part: strong thick hands, a weather-beaten face, eyes used to focusing on the horizon.

"In a manner of speaking, but the fishing I do is different now. I'm a priest."

I coughed in surprise. "A *priest*?"

He nodded and offered his hand. "Father Bartholomew Azevedo, but I prefer to go by Bart."

I introduced myself, all the while keenly aware of the bottle of booze on my lap, as blatant as a picture of a naked woman. I wanted it to disappear.

I didn't know what to say to him, but he picked up the slack. "Yessir, it's been an interesting journey. Growing up in Galilee—scholarship to Harvard, playing football there—Peace Corps in Brazil—and then the seminary. Oh, and I also found the time to become a drunk along the way. All in all I've been incredibly lucky."

"Becoming a, uhm, drunk . . . you think of that as lucky too?"

"In a way. It made me humble. I used to be too prideful. It also brought me to AA, which was one of the best things that ever happened to me."

I braced myself. Some of Mom's friends are in AA and I can't stand them. I can't stand their giving sermons at the drop of a hat, or the way they yap about the Higher Power.

But Bart let it go. He shifted gears. "Are you a Catholic?"

I shook my head. "My father's Jewish, my mother's Episcopalian. Myself, I'm not much of anything."

"I wasn't either, for a long time. I grew up in a

devout family but I went to church just once in four years at Harvard, for a funeral. You look surprised."

"I thought priests and nuns knew what they wanted to do when they were young. I thought they had . . . what's it called, a vocation?"

"Vocations come at different points. In the seminary I knew men in their thirties and forties. They'd done all kinds of things. My best friend was a former Boston cop who'd worked in Homicide."

With that, he was off and running, talking about his fellow seminarians, who included an ex-cattle rancher, an ex-NHL goalie, and an ex-IRS agent. He had a million stories. It was fun to listen to him, and he didn't preach. The time passed quickly.

It wasn't just a monologue. He asked me all kinds of questions about my parents, my school, and my goals. He was the easiest man to talk to I'd ever met, even easier than Farnsworth. Much harder to bullshit than Farnsworth, though. I knew better than to try.

At some point I slipped the bottle into my jacket as casually as possible.

When we began the descent into Providence, he pulled out his wallet. He took out a business card and gave it to me. "Here, Jeff, I'd like for you to have this. Feel free to call me anytime."

"Thanks." There was printing on both sides. On the back of it was written

> God grant me the serenity
> To accept the things I cannot change,
> The courage to change the things I can,
> And the wisdom to know the difference.

He saw me reading. "The Serenity Prayer. I'm sure you've heard it. Important to us in AA."

I felt myself tense up. Then I started to say something, to defend myself, even though he hadn't attacked me. Or had he?

He gave me no chance to speak. "I meant what I said about calling me. Anytime. Collect, if need be."

"Why? I mean, you hardly know me, you've sat next to me on a plane for two hours."

"Because I know a kindred soul when I meet one. I know that when someone drinks Yukon Jack straight from the bottle, alone, at 10:30 in the morning, he's not doing it for fun."

"That's not—you have to understand—"

"Just keep the card," he cut me off. "Use it when the time is right. Six months, a year, a couple of years from now. You'll know when."

The pilot got on the intercom, told us what the

weather was like in Providence and thanked us for flying Blah Blah Airlines. Bart and I said little more to each other, apart from good-bye and good luck. Somewhere in the back of my wallet I still have his card.

*   *   *

Dismissed by Odetta, I go back to my cell. The rest of the afternoon stretches ahead of me like a ribbon of highway across a desert.

I'm facing two felony counts of drug-related charges and three misdemeanors. Add up the time and it comes to twelve years max. I think how a single afternoon is endless, and I multiply it by several thousand, and suicide is starting to look good again.

Sleep, the only answer. I lie down, shut my eyes, try to block out the din. But falling asleep is only part of the problem. The other part is dreaming. The same dream, over and over and over:

I'm in the van again, the sheriff's van used to bring prisoners to and from court. I've just been arraigned. There are four of us going back to jail. Myself, two blacks, a Chicano. A double mesh partition separates us from the COs up front. They have the radio blasting, a reggae station. It's too loud for them to hear what's going on in back.

I rest my head against the side of the van and try to catnap. Big mistake. A fist slams into my face, a foot lurches up to catch me in the solar plexus. Before I have a chance to do anything, even catch my breath, a hand slips around my mouth. I start to bite, but when I do, the fingers grab and twist my lips like pliers.

I try to wriggle away from them, try to swing my arms, try to kick, but they're all over me. In no time I'm on the floor of the van, and my pants are down around my knees. No one says a word. The only things I hear are my own muffled screams, and the reggae.

One of them rams himself inside me, pounding, thrusting. It feels like he's ripping me in two. The pain is bad, but the sense of powerlessness is worse. There is absolutely nothing I can do to stop them. I don't pass out, not quite, but I fall into a kind of shock. The pain continues to be real, but there's a distance between me and it. Like, this is happening to someone else, although I know it isn't.

The man hunched over me grunts and finally gives out a curt little laugh, more like a hiss. The pain eases, but only for a moment. Another one is in me, and it's the same thing all over again, and then another.

The trip from court to jail takes twenty minutes,
during which they did it to me three more times.

I give up the attempt to sleep, lest I dream again,
and sit on the bed. For want of something better to do
I read the walls, which are filled with graffiti. Spurting
cocks, and naked women with gaping slits. *FUCK*
EVERYBODY! Swastikas. Garbled pieces of the Bible:
BUT I WAS LIKE A LAMB LED TO THE SLAWTER &
THEY HAD DEVISED DEVICES AGAINST ME. Drawings of broken hearts and fractured faces. Incomprehensible words and phrases: *FIGNOG, BOGENFOGER,*
BERCAN REIGNS! Pleas for help. Drawings of birds
and flowers. *ROBERTO CLEMENTE LIVES!* An American flag, upside down. *ELVIS LIVES!* And, above the
sink, in tiny, perfect letters, almost calligraphy: *it wasn't*
supposed to turn out like this.

I've spent hours staring at this stuff, wondering
about the ones who've written it. Who are they, where
are they now, what happened to them? Some of them
were clearly off the deep end. Were they crazy because
of drugs or were they crazy to begin with? How many
are out? How many of them are dead already? I imagine
that some of them died of AIDS. For all I know, I might
join them.

Martinez runs his keys across the bars and jars me back to the present. "Hey, Zwerling, get up. You got a visit."

"Who?" My lawyer's not supposed to come again for three more days.

He opens my cell door. "Your father."

*   *   *

The visiting room here isn't like the TV version where you talk by phone to your visitor as you sit on opposite sides of a thick glass window. It's basically a converted gym filled with long narrow tables. COs stand to the rear. They afford us more privacy than you'd expect. Unless you're on special precautions, you're allowed to have physical contact, to a point. Not that I want to have contact with anyone, not even to shake hands.

I'm given the number of the table beforehand. He's already there.

Doctor Zwerling has seen better days. His eyes are red, his face drawn and bloodless, his hair greasy and uncombed. His clothes are rumpled, as though he slept in them. He looks five years older than when I saw him last, six months ago. If he looks this bad to me, I can't imagine how I must look to him.

He reaches for my hand. I pull it away. A couple of times he tries to speak but his voice fades to a whisper. Finally, with stupendous effort, he says hello.

"Hi, Dad."

"Jesus Christ . . ." The voice fades off again.

"Listen, Dad, I'm sorry. I'm sorry I'm here, I'm sorry you ever had to see me here. I'm sorry about everything."

"Me too. I'm sorry I didn't"—he gropes for words— "pay more attention."

"Does Mom know?"

He nods. "We talked last night for almost an hour. She's flying here today, her plane's due in this evening."

He folds his hands in front him, on the table. When he speaks again, his voice is calmer, stronger, more doctorly. "Now, Jeff, I have the name of a lawyer here. I'm going to meet with him in two hours. We'll talk about bail, among other things. With luck we'll have you out of here tomorrow, possibly tonight. You'll put all of this behind you." Bravado. He doesn't believe it for a minute.

I interrupt him. "Did Odetta tell you what happened in the van?"

He lurches back as if I've punched him. And then he starts to cry, without a sound, the tears sliding down his unshaven cheeks. I've never seen him cry before. We are both acutely embarrassed.

Suddenly I feel very young, more like twelve than twenty. I feel the way I did when I was flying back and forth between New Mexico and Rhode Island, and we found ourselves in the midst of a storm, and the plane bounced around in the sky like a Whiffle ball. I want to be taken care of. I want to give up this stupid fucking pretense that I'm a grown-up.

Goddamn, he won't stop crying. I can't stand seeing him like this, I have to find some neutral subject, fast. Tough to do. With Dad and me there are so few of them.

There's a long awkward pause. "Listen, Dad," I say at last, "do you remember those deep-sea fishing trips we took when I was little?"

He looks surprised, then nods. "We'd leave from Galilee or Point Judith, spend the whole day on the water. You loved every minute, even when we didn't catch a thing. I've never seen you happier than you were on those trips."

A good topic, safe. I keep it going. "Sometimes I'll shut my eyes and remember every detail of them. The way the boat pitched, the way the sun beat down on us, the way the sea breeze felt against my face."

He smiles, to my huge relief. "I'll never forget the

first time you caught a blue. You weren't more than eight. It took you ten minutes to bring him in, but you stayed with him, you wouldn't give up. I was very proud of you . . . I was usually proud of you back then. You were so excited; you literally jumped up and down on the boat!"

"If I ever get out this hole, do you think we could go on another fishing trip for old time's sake?"

"I'd like that. You don't know how much."

Then neither of us says anything, but at least it's a more comfortable silence than the last one. He's dry-eyed now. It's good to see him, I admit to myself, in spite of everything.

He reaches for my hand again. This time I don't pull back.

SOUL MATE

Thou away art present still with me;
For thou not farther than my thoughts canst move,
And I am still with them, and they with thee—
Shakespeare, *47th Sonnet*

I MET HER on a Tuesday in April, when a light rain came & went all morning & the sun hid behind sheets of clouds. An ordinary day, at least that's how it seemed at first. Not a day to turn our lives completely upside down, to bind the 2 of us together till the end of time. Six years ago it was, closer to 7, & it still seems as fresh & clear as last night's dream.

We met in the post office, talk about ordinary. She stood in line in front of me. A thin girl, 5'5" or 5'6". Dressed casually—gray sweatshirt, jeans & sneakers. Red hair down to her shoulders. Since she stood ahead of me, I only saw her back at first. But the line formed a right angle just before it reached the counter. As she turned, I got to see her face. Which was finely formed, with high cheekbones & a thin straight nose that turned up slightly at the tip. Big blue eyes.

She wasn't beautiful. Her eyes were too close together & her skin was a bit rough, as if she'd acne once, & her lips were too thin. Not beautiful but very pretty. I particularly liked the long red hair. It was all I could do to keep from running a finger through it, which is something I've never done before. To touch a girl's hair like that, I mean.

So there we stood, this red-headed girl & me, waiting in line. In a few seconds she'd reach the counter, buy stamps or whatever, & she'd leave. I had to make contact with her. Had to. But I didn't have a clue about how to do it. I'm not what you'd call smooth.

Without thinking, since I had no time to think, I bumped against her, very lightly. *Excuse me,* I said. She turned around, didn't say anything, but she smiled. The nicest smile I'd ever seen.

Something sparked in me, like a small explosion in my brain. It was as if my whole life beforehand had only been a preparation for that moment. From the way she smiled at me, I knew we were connected. It went beyond that. This may not make sense to you, but I knew that she'd been put on Earth for me alone. I knew it on the spot, without the smallest doubt. The red-haired girl was my soul mate.

She came to the counter, bought a sheet of stamps. Then—this had to be fate, how else to explain it—she tore off a stamp & put it on a letter she was mailing. The letter had her name & return address, printed on one of those stickers you get from charities. If I hadn't seen it, I'd never have known her name or where she lived.

Her name was Karen Marsh. We had the same initials (my name is Keith Mueller). More proof that this was fate! She lived at 81 W. Lincoln Ave., Apt. 22. That's only about a mile from me.

As I walked out, I felt better than I'd felt in months or maybe years. I would have skipped along the pavement if it hadn't been for my limp.

When I got home, I thought right away about cleaning up the place, rearranging things to make it nicer for when she came over. My apartment is three rooms above a Greek restaurant. Most of the furniture came from my parents' home. Comfortable but not exactly fancy, except for my father's leather recliner. I never went in for much decoration, except for oil paintings on black velvet I got at a street fair, 2 for $50. One of Elvis, the other of a crying clown. I prefer the crying clown. It's deeper.

I could have afforded a bigger, nicer place to live, but this one was okay for me. My needs were pretty modest. I lived alone except for the goldfish, Norm & Norma, & Lulu the parakeet. Money was no problem. As the sole survivor of a car accident when I'd turned 19, when a drunk driver killed my parents & sister, I inherited everything. Including the stocks & bonds for my father's retirement, worth $450,000. There was also money from the court case against the drunk driver. After I paid the lawyer, it came to about a million & a half. Of course the accident had its drawbacks. I lost an eye, & I broke a leg in three places. The doctor said I'll always limp. Not to mention, my memory & concentration aren't the best, & I get irritable, & I get more than my share of headaches. Post-concussion syndrome, it's called.

I thought about Karen all that day. I imagined going to the beach with her, walking hand in hand, & taking her to fancy restaurants, the kind with candles on the table & the menu's in French, even though I don't know French. I imagined bringing her to my apartment, which I decided to refurnish & maybe get new paintings. I imagined her meeting Lulu & the goldfish. Then, a few months later, I'd give her an engagement ring. I'd do it in one of our fancy restaurants, after ordering champagne which I'd never had before.

Our wedding would be a small affair. What was left of my family, mainly a couple of uncles, aunts & cousins, & her immediate family. I wouldn't have to worry about inviting friends since I don't have any. I'd let her have a few of hers if she really wanted them, but not more than 4 or 5. We'd go someplace nice for the honeymoon. Niagara Falls, or maybe Bermuda, which would be more expensive but it's supposed to be great for honeymoons. Romantic & so forth.

Then we'd come home & everything would be perfect. The honeymoon would go on forever. We'd be the happiest couple in the world. Within a day of meeting her, I'd worked out the rest of our lives.

Too bad my parents wouldn't be around to see it. But they wouldn't have believed it anyway. They wouldn't have believed their son could get a girl like that. Their dimwit son with his bad grades & his nervous tic, their scapegoat.

But it hadn't been just my parents. Fact was, people never went out of their way to treat me well. Other kids picked on me. The rest of the family, my uncles, aunts & so forth, lived far away. My grandparents too, the two of them who were still alive when I was born. When we managed to get together—once every couple of years, whenever—they mostly ignored me. So did neighbors, so did teachers.

Except for Ms. Gleiss.

*   *   *

Lisa Gleiss was my high school English teacher. Best teacher I ever had, the only one who took an interest in me. She was young, 27 or 28, but she had an older air about her. Maybe it was how she dressed, always in black & navy blue. Funny how she wouldn't wear bright colors. Tall, close to 6 feet. Thin, not much of a bosom. Dark hair tied up in a bun. Huge black eyes, the prettiest thing about her. When she looked at you, she seemed to take in everything about you.

The first week of class she told us to write a book report. The book was called *Animal Farm* by someone named George Orwell. Books were never much to me, but this one I kind of liked. Short & simple, & I liked reading about the talking animals.

I wrote a 2-page report the night before it was due, since I always did homework at the last moment. When I got it back, she'd covered the pages with comments. It looked as if she wrote as much as I did. She ended her comments with a note. *Please see me after class.*

We met the next day. I had no idea what to expect as I stood fidgeting by her desk. She pointed to a chair—*Sit down, Keith. Relax, I won't bite.* Then she smiled, which caught me by surprise since she didn't often smile. I saw she was joking. But it wasn't a mean joke, the way they usually were.

Then we talked. She asked me what I thought about the book, & told me how writers could use stories to express their political opinions, & explained about satire, which I'd never heard of. She said my writing showed promise but I'd have to work on it. *She said my writing showed promise.* No one ever told me I'd showed promise about anything.

In all, she spent half an hour with me.

She met with me as often as she could. Once every couple of weeks, on average. She talked about books, how much she loved them, & she recommended all kinds of them. Aside from that, she asked me about myself & my family. She even told me about her own life, which no teacher had done. She told me she had an older brother & younger sister, & how she sometimes felt lost between them. She told me about her father dying of some blood disease when she was in college &

how she still hadn't gotten over it although it happened 8 years ago. He was the one she'd been closest to.

For the first & only time in school I showed some effort. I read the extra things she suggested, mainly for her approval. I still remember some of them. One of them, *The Catcher in the Rye*, about a boy my age, not real happy either. Another, *The Old Man & the Sea*, because I told her I hoped to go fishing someday. Another, *Of Mice & Men*, about some retard & his friend. In class I paid attention to everything she said. I took part in discussions, which I'd never done before. I did homework on time. My writing got better, just the way she said it would. Ms. Gleiss gave me an *A*. Only one I ever got.

In a few months, Lisa Gleiss became the most important person in my life. Apart from my favorite teacher, she became my closest friend. But what we had was more than friendship. I thought about her morning, noon & night. I wished I could be with her all the time, not just in the classroom. I wondered what it would be like to live with her instead of my parents & sister. I didn't even have the tics when I was with her!

I don't know when I began to think of marrying her. At first it was only a daydream. The more I thought about it, though, it didn't seem so odd. She was 12 years older, but so what? Men marry younger women every day, so who says women shouldn't marry younger men? Soon I'd worked out everything. I'd get a job, wouldn't have to be a great one. If all else failed, I'd work at a fast food place or pump gas. Between that & her teaching, we'd get by. Maybe I'd even take some college courses. Before Ms. Gleiss I'd never given college a second thought.

We'd live in her apartment until we saved enough to buy a house, somewhere near the city's outskirts, with lots of land around it. Not a fancy one, we didn't need a mansion, but warm & cozy. We wouldn't go out except to work & shop for food & so forth. Once in a while, we'd take a walk together. Just the 2 of us, although I might let her have a pet if she really wanted one. Who could say, we might even have children someday. I'd have to think about it, though.

I was too shy to tell her all that, but no matter. In the end we'd be together. Meanwhile, this was the happiest I'd been. I didn't know the term back then, but I began to think of her as my soul mate.

Then, one day in March, after class, she dropped a bomb. *I have something to tell you, Keith. I won't be here next year.*

My mouth became too dry for me to talk. *Why not?*

I finally asked her. Then she explained about going back to school. To graduate school, to get something called a Ph.D. She'd be 2,000 miles away.

You can't go. You're the best teacher I've ever had. You can't leave me. Stupidest thing I ever said. She could go where she wanted, she could do what she pleased.

She smiled that sad sweet smile of hers. *Listen, Keith* . . . But I didn't hear any more. I practically ran out of the room. It would have been the last straw to let her see me cry while I sat there, crushed.

After that, I barely cracked a book, never said a thing in class. In time she stopped calling on me. The school year ended & I never saw or heard from her again. I'll admit, it took me awhile to get over her. Maybe I didn't, not fully, until Karen.

At one point I made a vow to myself. If I ever cared about another woman, *really* cared about her, I'd never let her get away.

*   *   *

Back to Karen. The problem was how to get to know her.

If she had a listed number I could phone her. Or I

could show up where she lived. Or I could write to her. Just showing up was too direct, I thought, even though we were soul mates. A letter might do the trick, but I don't write very good ones. I decided on a phone call.

I looked in the phone book. Sure enough, I found a listed number for K. Marsh on W. Lincoln. So I decided on the spot to call her that evening. Just thinking about it made my heart race!

For supper I had my favorite frozen dinner, fried chicken, in honor of the occasion, & a shot of Old Grand Dad for courage. Then I called her, although I wasn't clear on what I'd say. Sometimes I get tongue-tied. I'll admit, I was relieved in spite of myself when I got her answering machine. *Hi, this is Karen . . . I can't come to the phone right now . . . Leave your name and number at the beep, and I'll get back to you . . .*

I loved her voice, which was businesslike but warm & a little flirty. I knew she knew I'd call her, & I knew she'd left the message for me alone. I loved her voice, in fact I already loved everything about her.

I thought about leaving a message, but I didn't. I wanted to talk to her directly, without an answering machine between us. But even though I didn't leave a message, I called her back 10 times, just to hear her voice.

On Thursday morning I set the alarm for 7:00, even though I didn't have to go to work until 11:30. I had a part-time job at a video place, 25 hours per week. My salary wasn't much, but I didn't need it anyway. The main thing was, a job filled up some time.

If I called her early enough, I might catch her before she left for work. My heart beat like crazy while the phone rang, the way it did the night before. And she answered!

Hello—? Her voice was thick & sleepy.

Trying to think of things to say to her, I froze. *Hello,* she said again. She sounded a tiny bit impatient. Again, I said nothing, but my breathing sounded pretty loud.

Is this the person who made those hang-up calls? She sounded angry now, & maybe frightened. I should have told her she had nothing to be frightened of, but I didn't. Then there was a long pause, or maybe it just seemed long, & she finally said *Please—stop—calling— me.* She pronounced each word slowly & distinctly, as if she spoke to someone who didn't know English very well.

Of course I knew she didn't mean it.

A few moments later I hung up. I had to admit, we weren't off to a real good start. But so what? All the great lovers had problems. Look at Romeo & Juliet, or O.J. & Nicole.

Later, it occurred to me that I needed to find out more about her. Where she worked, what she liked & so forth. I didn't know exactly what I wanted to find out, but I wanted to find out as much as possible. The best way would be to hire someone to do it for me.

I went through the Yellow Pages. There were 2 pages of listings for private detectives. I picked the one nearest me, Peerless Investigative Services. Close enough to walk there. I have a car, a 3-yr.-old Ford Victoria, not stylish but solid, puts lots of metal between the road & me. Ever since the accident I haven't liked to drive. I'd rather walk or take a bus.

Peerless's office was 20 minutes away, in a run-down red brick building. The bricks were grimy, most of them closer to black than red. Several offices looked empty, with boarded-up windows. When I finally got off the elevator, which took forever to go up 3 floors, I sat in a waiting room with wooden chairs & a few issues of *People*, one of them a year old.

A man came out of the inner office when he heard me come in. About my height, 5'11", but he weighed more than I do, at least 230. Greasy thick dark hair. A nose tilting to one side, probably broken once. He wore a brown striped sweater, too tight for him. He introduced himself, no handshake. His name was John Jarrett.

He brought me to the inner office & sat behind a desk with so much junk that you could hardly see the surface. The rest of the room was cluttered too, full of file cabinets & bookcases. The bookcases held piles of manila folders, photography equipment & binoculars. A computer terminal sat on its own table.

I parked myself in front of his desk in another wooden chair & he got right down to business. *Okay, Mr. Mueller, how can I help you?* Rasping voice of a heavy smoker. I forgot to mention, he had an overflowing ashtray on the desk.

I'd like to find out some things about someone, I told him.

What kind of things?

Where she works. What she does in her spare time. Anything you can.

He looked me over as he played with a rubber band. *What's her name?*

Karen Marsh. I gave him the address & phone number.

Why do you want to know about her?

I'd prepared for that. He might not have understood if I told him I met her in the post office 2 days ago, hadn't even spoken to her.

We met in Florida last year. In a bar. We both drank quite a bit. Truthfully, I don't remember much. But I remember liking her, & wanting to get to know her, & I think she liked me too. Last week, going through some papers, I found one with her name & number—thought I'd lost it. Well, I want to contact her, but first I want to find out more about her. Like whether or not she's married, where she works & so forth. As much as I can.

It must have sounded pretty lame.

He jotted notes & resumed playing with the rubber band. *I'll find out what I can,* he said finally. *I charge $90 an hour, plus expenses, with a $500 retainer.*

I took a check from my wallet & wrote it out. He studied it carefully & nodded. It occurred to me, he didn't believe a word I said, about meeting her in Florida & so forth. But it didn't matter to him as long as he got the money.

The next week John Jarrett called me & told me to come in again. It turned out he'd learned a fair bit about her. *Twenty-six years old, single, managed a shop called Candles & More at the Somerset Mall. Drove a blue Honda Civic, two years old, license plate LVZ 944. Graduated*

*from a local high school, Southeast Regional. Two-year
degree in retailing from a community college. Had lived
with a man named John Mihaliak for 18 months but now
it was just her and a cat. Excellent credit, paid her bills
on time. Registered Democrat. Vegetarian. Worked out
at the Alpha Sports & Racquet Club, where she also did
Jazzercise & took kick-boxing.*

He said her birthday was 10/6. More proof that we
were fated for each other! My birthday is 6/10!

One thing I've learned through all this, anyone can
find out anything about anyone.

*   *   *

The next decision, how best to use this information? I shied away from a direct encounter, at least for a
while, since the phone calls hadn't gone too well, but I
could pave the way for later.

What better way to do that than with flowers?

First, I bought a mixed arrangement, looked real
nice, very colorful. I had them delivered to her home,
no note. She'd know they were from me anyway. A few
days later I sent a dozen red roses to the candle shop.
This time I did include a note. *We'll meet soon. Until
then.* A few days after that I sent a dozen yellow ones

to the Alpha. *Love Always,* the note said. Then I sent a bunch of red & white carnations to the candle shop again. I had them attach a heart-shaped balloon, shiny red. The note said *I'm yours forever.* Each time I used a different flower shop & I always paid cash.

At this point I was almost ready for a face-to-face encounter with her, now that she'd been softened up. I needed to see her urgently, I was thinking of her day & night.

I began to spend time at the mall, which had benches in the corridors. There was one outside the candle shop. No one minded if I sat there as long as I wanted. I watched as she waited on customers, rang up sales & chatted with the other girls who worked there. Sometimes men tried to strike up a conversation with her, which made me angry. One of them really seemed to be taken with her, pestering her for a good 10 minutes. It got hard for me to control myself. I almost went in to set him straight, if you know what I mean.

I didn't see any of the flowers I sent to her. I'll admit, that disappointed me, but I forgave her.

Also, I began to check out where she lived. Lincoln was a quiet street, mainly with small apartment buildings. Hers was U-shaped, 3 stories, courtyard in the front. By the side of the building a driveway led to tenants' parking spaces in back. Late one night, closing up the video store, I walked over. I'd bought a book of love poems from a Barnes & Noble. When I found her Honda Civic, I put the book beneath the windshield wiper.

She had a set routine, & it was easy to get the hang of it. Every morning, at 8, she let the cat out. The candle shop opened at 10 (noon on Sundays), & she usually left home about 9:30. Before she left, she let the cat back in. The shop stayed open until 7, but she didn't always work that late. On Tuesdays & Fridays she left early. Those were the afternoons she went to the Alpha. Thursday was her longest day, when the shop stayed open until 9:30. She took Monday off.

If she went in to work late, she spent most mornings at home. Or she ran errands, shopping & so forth. She used a supermarket about 4 blocks from her apartment. (I followed her there a few times. Once I was right behind her in the checkout line!) Tuesday evenings she liked to go to the movies with a girl who lived in the same building.

I forgot to mention, I'd begun to take photos of her. I bought a Canon, easy to get used to. A good thing, since I hadn't done photography before. It even had a zoom lens, so I could shoot from a distance.

By early June I figured we were ready for the next

phase. Time to write to her. She really gave me no choice, since she'd changed to an unlisted telephone number.

*   *   *

Dearest Karen, I began.

Do you remember when we met, in April? I guess it's fixed in your memory forever, like it's fixed in mine. We were at the post office, waiting together in the line. I was behind you. At one point you turned & smiled at me. We connected, on the spot, as I've never connected with another person. Nor have you, I'm certain.

Since then, I've thought about you constantly. You're the first thing I think about when I wake up & the last thing before I fall asleep. I imagine how it will be when we're together. How it will be when we have dinner together & clean up afterwards (you wash, I'll dry!) How it will be to take walks & watch TV. How it will be to go to bed, snuggled against each other.

I have money, so you won't have to work at the candle shop anymore. In fact we'll barely have to leave the house at all, except to get groceries & food for your cat & so forth. We'll be a world unto ourselves, bound together until the end of time.

Love always, Keith

It took me half the night to write it, to get it absolutely right. Two days later, I wrote another one.

Dearest Karen,

Last night, in bed, thinking of you before I fell asleep the way I always do, it occurred to me that you don't know anything about me yet. That isn't right since I already know a few things about you. Where you went to school, & how you lived with John, & how you're a vegetarian—things like that. Well, you should know a bit about me too, so here goes.

I'm a year younger than you. Only 8 months, really, since your birthday's in October & mine's in June. My parents are dead, my sister too. They all died in the same accident. I'd be lying if I said I missed them much, especially my sister. She was older, & she always hated me. It was mutual. Stuck up, thought she was queen of the world because she made good grades & had friends (myself, I was pretty much a loner). She liked to roll up a magazine & hit me with it, the way you hit a dog that makes a mess. That leaves no mark, so she could play Miss Innocence. When I tried to hit her back, she ran squealing to our parents. They always took her side. I have to admit, she was pretty. But not as pretty as you are!

Let's see, what else. My grades were nothing to brag about. I wasn't a great athlete either. Sports bored me, still do. But if you're a sports fan, that's okay.

I like to stay at home when I'm not working. You too, I'll bet. But if you want to go out occasionally, to see your friends & so forth, that's okay too. As long as it doesn't take away too much of our time together. Which reminds me. I plan to buy some exercise equipment for our apartment. An exercise bike & treadmill to start with. That way you can exercise at home. Which means that we'll be together more. And you'll be able to give up your membership at the Alpha. Those places are too expensive anyway.

Well, that's it for now. I close this letter with 1,000,000 kisses & cannot wait until I'm lying next to you, running my fingers through your hair, & becoming One with you.

Love always, Keith

Dearest Karen, I wrote, a week later.

Sometimes, although we haven't met yet (not officially), I feel such a strong connection to you that I can hardly put it into words.

My guess is, you've had a hard life too. Your face is lovely, but there's sadness in it. There's so much talk of child abuse now. Common as measles, just about. In my heart, I know you were abused. I see it in your eyes.

When I think of that, I want to take you in my arms & comfort you. I also want to teach a lesson to those who've hurt you. Someday I will & that's a promise.

I understand everything you've been through. Your pain is mine, & mine is yours. Together we'll make our way through it. We'll hold each other, & the pain will finally go away. What they've done to us won't matter. You & me against the world. That's how it'll be, forever.

Love always, Keith

I waited a few more days. Then, at last, I was ready to meet her face to face. It was time.

But something else happened.

*   *   *

One morning I woke up to a loud rapping on my door. It was early, before 8. I thought it might be the police but could think of no reason why they'd bother me. I'd done nothing wrong.

I threw on a robe & went to the door, which has a peephole. Looking through it, I saw two men. Not friendly. One of them was close to me in age, the other about 50. The younger one was tall, about 6'2", with a reddish crew cut & blue eyes that looked familiar although I knew we hadn't met. He wore khakis & a black T-shirt that showed off the muscles of his upper arms & shoulders. Weight-lifter type.

What do you want? I asked.

We want to talk to you about Karen, said the older one. He was shorter, maybe 5'11". Bald. Bit of a potbelly, but with a pretty solid look about him too.

I took deep breaths to calm myself & forced myself to keep my hands from shaking.

Let us in, said the younger one. He said it in a way that didn't make you want to argue. I opened the door, mainly because I thought they'd knock it down if I didn't.

Who are you? I asked as they stood next to me, one on each side.

I'm Karen's father, the older one answered in a cold tight voice. He nodded towards the younger one. *That's her brother, Patrick.*

Karen? Who's that? I paused, pretending to try to remember. *I don't know a Karen.*

Don't get cute with us, Mister, or you'll be spitting out your teeth, the younger one spoke for the first time. *Karen Marsh. The one you've stalked for the last 2 months.*

*The one you made those hang-up calls to, until she
changed her number. The one you sent these letters to,
you twisted fuck,* her father added. He pulled my letters
from a pocket & waved them at me.

I don't know what you're talking about, I said, trying
to sound indignant. As a matter of fact, I *was* indignant.
Who were *they* to come into my home & talk to me that
way?

We know who you are, the older one ignored me.
*Think you're the only one who knows how to get the
goods on someone? I was a cop for 30 years. We know all
about you. Keith Mueller, age 26. High school dropout,
works part time at Meadowbrook Video. Never married,
no girlfriend. Total loser. Came into money when your
parents died, otherwise you wouldn't have a dime.*

The younger stepped towards me. His face was so
close that I could smell the eggs & coffee on his breath.
*Better listen to us, Mister. She doesn't want your flowers
or your goddamn poetry books. She doesn't want you
coming to the store or hanging around where she works
out. She especially doesn't want you anywhere near her
apartment. She wants nothing to do with you, not now,
not a year from now, not ever. DO YOU THINK YOU'VE
GOT THAT STRAIGHT?*

The older one spoke more calmly. *Of course, she*

could get a restraining order. That means you'd be arrested if you set foot near her, or sent her something at the store, or even if you wrote her one of your horse-shit letters. I've checked you out. It's obvious you're an asshole, but at least you don't have a record. See, guys like you don't do well in jail. They wind up as punching bags or someone's girlfriend. But that's irrelevant, since Karen doesn't need a restraining order, does she? Because my son & me will come down on you like gangbusters if you ever, EVER, try to contact her again.

You're already down to one eye, the younger one threw in. *How'd you like to lose the other one? Accidents happen.*

I was scared, but angry too. *I think you better leave now. If you don't, I'll call 911.*

The younger one was in my face again, close enough for him to sink his teeth into me. *Yeah, you do that, Mister. We'll help you dial.*

I went into the kitchen when they left. Took out the Old Grand Dad, poured myself a double shot. First time I ever drank so early. Then I settled back into my father's recliner, where I like to do my serious thinking.

At first I was too mad to think. I've never hated anyone as much as them. Hated them more than the kids who teased me about the tics. More than my pediatrician, Dr. Rue, who touched me in the wrong places when his nurse left the examining room. More than my parents, even more than my sister.

Then the bourbon began to calm me, & I began to think more clearly. The first thing that occurred to me, it wasn't *Karen's* fault. I was sure she'd never gotten so much love & attention from a man. Which meant she wasn't used to it. Maybe it even frightened her. So she'd turned to the father & brother, & they'd poisoned her against me. It made perfect sense.

What happened was *their* fault. Entirely. They'd probably tried to control her all her life, to keep her to themselves. *They* were the ones who'd abused her. Sneaking into her bedroom late at night, doing awful things to her, & then trying to keep her from true happiness with someone else, namely me. That's what happened, I was certain. Since she was blameless, I decided to forgive her.

As I sat in the recliner & finished off the bourbon, something else occurred to me. I had *rights*. It might be better if I did back off, at least for awhile, but in the end I could contact her if I wanted to. It was still a free country.

Who knows, something might even happen to one of them. Like Patrick said, accidents happen.

*   *   *

I didn't see her for a month. Didn't write her, didn't send her flowers or anything else. That was hard, not sending gifts. I often window-shopped, looking at things I knew she'd like. A leather purse, or a gold necklace, & so forth. If I saw things I really thought she'd like, I bought them anyway. I bought them to save for the day when we'd be together. Soon they filled half a closet. Some of them cost a fortune, but so what. Who better to spend money on than your soul mate?

One morning, in August, after I fed Norm & Norma, I let Lulu out of her cage. She needed to stretch her wings from time to time & fly around the apartment. As I watched the goldfish, with Lulu darting over us, I suddenly remembered—*Karen had a cat!* That would cause a major problem when we were finally a couple. Lulu & the goldfish wouldn't last a day with that stupid cat around!

I'll admit, I never cared for cats. They do nothing except lie around & sleep until it's time to feed them. They're not affectionate & loyal like dogs. Plus, their litter boxes stink, and their breath doesn't smell so great either. My sister had a cat, a nasty creature, black as midnight, who arched her back & hissed whenever I came near her. She would have scratched my eyes out if I gave her the chance.

I pondered the problem of Karen's cat. She liked her cat, no doubt about it. You could tell from the way she held it & petted it when she let it out. She'd miss it if something happened to it. I knew how bad I'd feel if something happened to Lulu or the goldfish.

On the other hand, she'd get over it. People get over worse things than losing a cat. She'd realize that it would have caused resentment on my part & driven a wedge between us. Not to mention what it would have done to Lulu, Norm & Norma!

Of course if Karen knew I had anything to do with her cat's disappearance, she might become annoyed with me. But why should she suspect it? Cats often leave & don't come back. I'd have to be very careful, though.

The first step was making sure Karen still held to her routine. I'd have to resume surveillance of her apartment. It would also give me a chance to see her again. About time! It had been 2 months!

The next morning I felt that same old thrill as I headed to her apartment. I parked on the other side of the street from her building, not directly across from it, just close enough for me to see the entrance. Sure enough, at 8 on the dot she let the cat out.

I strained to get a look at her, wishing I had binoculars. Her hair was shorter now, to just below her ears, probably shortened for the summer. Otherwise she looked the same. I couldn't see her eyes (she had on sunglasses), but I'd have recognized her anywhere. She wore denim cutoffs & a tank top. First time I'd seen her wearing shorts & she looked good in them. Nice legs, very trim & muscular. Those hours at the Alpha had paid off for her.

Later that week, I bought different cans of cat food. Cats are real fussy about their eating. I remember that from the one my sister had. If you gave her a kind she didn't like, she'd walk off in a huff. I also bought a box of catnip & a carrying case of hard plastic, the kind used to bring pets to the vet.

I knew it would be dangerous. If her windows overlooked the courtyard & she glanced out the window at the wrong time, it could ruin everything. And if she saw me, no telling what could happen. She might call the cops, or the father & brother, which would be worse. There was also the chance that someone might see me taking off with the cat & tell her about it later. Unlikely, though. Most of the tenants left for work from the back of the building where their cars were parked. It would be a risky business, but sometimes you have to overlook the risks & take them anyway.

Ninety minutes between her letting out the cat & letting it back in. Ninety minutes, that's all I had.

The next day it rained, but the day after that was clear & fair. I drove to her apartment, & I'm sure I looked calmer than I felt. The steering wheel was damp from my sweaty palms. Cans of cat food & so forth were on the passenger seat next to me.

She let the cat out, right on schedule. I waited 5 minutes before making my way to the courtyard. The courtyard had 2 trees, one on each side. I sat beneath one, pretending to be reading the paper.

Very quietly, almost whispering, I began to call it. *Here, kitty . . . here, kitty . . .* At first it ignored me. Too busy chasing squirrels. Then I opened one of the cans of cat food, the salmon. I put some on a paper plate & put the plate a couple of yards away from me. The cat got a little curious but went back to chasing squirrels. I opened up a second can, the chicken. This time I didn't put the paper plate so far away. The cat came close enough to sniff it. Still refused to eat it, though. Obviously a fussy spoiled one, like my sister's. So I opened up a third one, lamb & rice. Bingo!

After letting it eat awhile, I spread some catnip on the ground between the paper plate & me. Some of them like catnip & some don't, but I was lucky. This one really loved the stuff, rolling around in it with its eyes shut, purring. I reached over to pet it. As long as it still had the catnip, it didn't mind a bit.

I put some catnip in the carrying case, scooped up the cat with one quick move & shoved it in. Success! The cat hissed & tried to claw me, but I didn't let it. Only one thing left to do, to gather up the paper plates & cans. Then I headed to my car. The operation didn't take as much time as I expected. I checked my watch—under half an hour.

The cat meowed very loudly, in fact it yowled, but too bad! No one saw me as I opened the trunk & threw the case in.

In the car, I had rubber gloves, a kitchen knife with a sharpened blade, big plastic bags & electrician's tape. Plus, I had 2 bricks. I drove 10 miles past the city limits, to an isolated stretch of land by the river's edge that I'd checked out beforehand. This particular stretch was overrun with weeds, & people used parts of it as a dump. Except for a few fishermen, offshore in small boats, no one ever came there. After parking the Ford, I put on the rubber gloves, got the knife & took the cat out. I didn't want to hurt it unnecessarily, only to get rid of it as quickly & efficiently as possible. Just one slash across its neck, that's all it took. Bloody little bugger, though. I sure was glad I had the gloves on!

I put its body in the bags, one inside the other, which I weighed down with the bricks. I also threw in the bloody gloves. Then I sealed the whole thing up with electrician's tape. Taking one last look around, making sure that no one else was there, I hurled the bag as far from shore as I could manage.

Everything else I simply left. The carrying case, the cans of cat food & so forth. Like I said, people often dumped things there. A bit more clutter wouldn't matter or attract attention.

I drove back to the apartment, relieved & calm. Didn't have to be at work until 1:30, & it wasn't even noon. Plenty of time to shower, change clothes & fix myself a couple of sandwiches. Too many butterflies in my stomach to eat before I went to Karen's, & I was famished.

*   *   *

I closed the shop as usual that night after shelving all the video returns, preparing the bank deposit, neatening up & so forth. By the time I got home it was nearly 11. The restaurant downstairs was dark & no one stirred inside. It closes at 9:30 weeknights.

As I climbed the steps to my apartment, I felt uneasy, although I had no reason to. The building was very quiet, the way it usually is when the restaurant is closed. Only 3 apartments, all on the same floor. There's mine, & an old Greek widow lives in another one, & a young single guy lives in the 3rd one. But you hardly ever hear the old Greek lady, & the single guy spends most nights at his girlfriend's place.

I continued up the stairs. Still nothing out of the ordinary, but the uneasiness persisted. I couldn't wait to get into my own apartment. No place like home. My hand shook as I unlocked the door, but I felt better as soon as I stepped inside. I went over to the recliner without bothering to turn a light on. Sometimes it's nice to sit in the dark like that. Helps me unwind.

But the lights went on anyway! The brother stood on one side of me, the father on the other. I heard myself gasp, & every muscle in my body tightened. I wondered if I'd have a heart attack.

At first they said nothing, they just stared down at me, as if I were a snake or spider. The only things I heard were bubbles from the fish tank, & the 3 of us breathing,

& occasionally a passing car. The sounds were unnaturally clear, the way they are in dreams.

Where's the cat? her father asked me.

Cat? What cat? I have no idea what you're talking about.

Her brother lunged at me. He slapped my face so hard he jarred my teeth. So hard I thought he might knock over the recliner, which is practically impossible. It's a pretty solid chair.

He stepped back & stood with his legs a bit apart, hands on hips. *I'm warning you, Mister. Don't screw with us.*

Where's the cat? her father asked again.

What cat? Whose cat? I tried to sound confused & put upon.

The brother took a half a step towards me. He didn't slap me though, not this time. But you could tell he wanted to. *Whose do you think, asshole? Karen's, of course. She let him out this morning, the way she always does, & he never came back.*

She's had that cat for 5 years now, Karen's father chimed in. *He's got his habits, like most cats. Goes out in the morning, comes back before she goes to work.*

I tried to sound concerned. *Look, I'm sorry if it's lost or something. But things happen all the time to* cats. *My sister had a cat that someone poisoned.* I didn't mention that I'd done the poisoning. *They run away, they get hit by cars—*

Not this one, her brother interrupted. *He never ran away before, not once. We checked the streets around her place, we even checked the driveways. Guess what? No dead cats around.*

Then we thought of you, said Karen's father. *You're just the sort of sick fuck who'd hurt it for no reason. Funny, how that thought occurred to all of us.*

I rubbed my face, which still smarted. *Why would I want to hurt her cat?*

Well, that's a real good question, said her brother. *Who knows? To punish her because she wouldn't be your goddamn soul mate? To bring it back to her so you could be a hero, & that would make her care about you after all? Or, maybe you're so crazy that you did it for the hell of it.*

The 2 of them held all the cards, so I tried not to show my resentment. I particularly resented his telling me that I was crazy. I'd be the first to admit that I've had my problems, & my personality may be out of the ordinary, but I'm not crazy, never have been. I'm also smarter than people think. Especially when my back's against the wall.

I quickly went over the morning, again. Unless one of Karen's neighbors happened to glance out a window at the wrong time, no one saw me take off with the cat. I was sure of that. Which meant her father & brother had nothing to go on. They could suspect me & accuse me, but they had no witnesses. No evidence either. The only evidence would have been the cat itself, & the cops weren't about to drag the river for it.

You can beat me up if it'll make you happy, I told them, *but I didn't hurt her cat*. I tried to sound calmer than I felt.

You may have noticed that I have animals myself, I went on. *A parakeet & 2 goldfish. I love animals. Fact is, I'd rather die than hurt one.*

They said nothing, but it wasn't hard to read their minds. They were trying to decide if they believed me. The brother was more inclined to, even though he'd been the one who hit me.

We really don't have any proof, Dad, he said finally.

I don't need proof. He did it & that's that. I'd stake my life on it.

Frisky could have just taken off, the way the Andersons' cat did last summer, the brother argued. He wanted to believe me. I could tell.

The father shook his head. *This jerk-off busts into*

her life, & the next thing you know, her cat disappears. It's too much of a coincidence. But even he began to have some doubts.

Frisky might still come back, the son said. *He's been gone for less than a day. Hell, he might even be back now.*

The father shook his head again. *She would have called us on the cell.* I kept quiet while they hashed it out. The less I said, the better. Finally, the father moved slightly closer to me & rested his hand on my shoulder. If you hadn't known what happened earlier, you might have taken it for a friendly gesture.

I know you did something to that cat, he said. *All those years on the force, I learned to trust my instincts. We all did, if we wanted to stay alive. But Patrick's right. There's no proof, at least not yet, which makes you a very lucky guy. You better pray to God we don't find any. If we do, you're gonna wish that you were never born.* He turned & headed slowly towards the door, the brother a few steps behind him.

The next morning I called Jordan Barker. Mr. Barker was a partner at Rossi, Drummond, & Barker, the lawyers who took care of my parents' wills & so forth. They also handled the suit against the drunk driver. Only firm our family used. Old Man Rossi, the senior partner, dead now, had been my grandfather's lawyer 50 years ago.

Mr. Barker saw me that same day. I knew he would. It didn't matter whether or not he liked me. In fact he probably didn't. The thing is, we'd been good customers. He must have made over $300,000 just from the case against the drunk. There was also the money from my parents' wills, & setting up a trust fund, & all the family business that came earlier.

If he didn't like me, at least he tried to hide it. When I met with him that afternoon, he flashed this big phony smile at me, like a TV game show host. We shook hands, & he pumped my arm as if I'd been a long-lost relative.

Mr. Barker was in his 40s, but you might have pegged for 33 or 34. He's at least 6'4" & well-built, a former college basketball player who kept in shape. Brown wavy hair, dark eyes, trim mustache. Dressed to kill, as usual. That afternoon he wore a gray suit that fit him like a second skin, a red & blue print tie, & a white shirt with silver cufflinks.

His office wasn't too much smaller than my whole apartment. A family of 6 could have used his desk for a dinner table. On the walls he'd hung some modern paintings. They didn't impress me much. Basically just splotches of color.

I sat down in one of his leather chairs & we made small talk for awhile. Then he turned to business. *Well, Keith, what brought you here?*

It's kind of a long story . . . I began at the end, telling how the father & brother of a woman I knew broke into my apartment & ambushed me when I came home from work last night. How Patrick hit me (the bruise was still visible). How they accused me of hurting Karen's cat—I tried to sound indignant. How they threatened me.

Then I backed up & told him about me & Karen. How we met one day at the post office & I liked her immediately, & how I thought she felt the same about me. How I'd sent her flowers, a reasonable thing to do when you like someone, especially when you're shy. How I still hoped we'd go out someday. But I didn't tell him about our being soul mates. He wouldn't have understood.

Mr. Barker scribbled on his yellow pad. Every so often he looked up at me, very serious. He had a load of questions. Had I ever seen them before? How could they have gotten into my apartment? (I told him I had no idea, which was true.) Were there any witnesses? Could the neighbors have overheard us? Had I asked them to leave? Had they carried weapons? Had they left any evidence behind them, any proof that they were there? Had *I* said or done anything which they might have interpreted as threatening? Had I ever threatened Karen? Had I actually talked to her? Had she talked to me? Had she asked me *not* to contact her? (I suppose you could say so, after I made those hang-up calls, but why confuse him?)

His questions changed, & he began to ask me about myself. How was I doing, how did I feel? How did I spend my time? Was I working? What kind of a job, how many hours? How long had I worked there? Was I still having problems from the accident, bad nerves & so forth? Did I take any nerve pills? Did I see a psychiatrist or psychologist? He seemed embarrassed when he asked me that one. It offended me that he thought I was a nut case, but I let it pass.

Had I had any problems with the law? I thought that one was pretty stupid. If so, he would have been the first to know.

He listened to me for over half an hour, asking questions, taking notes the whole time. When he finished, he played with his fountain pen, not saying anything. Finally, *You said you don't know the father's first name?* I shook my head.

It doesn't matter. A retired cop named Marsh, in his 50s, with a son & daughter named Patrick & Karen . . .

should be easy enough for our investigator to find out who he is.

He put the pen down. *Well, Keith, we have some options here. I could call the DA's office, ask him to issue warrants. Breaking & entering, third degree assault & threatening. Add them up & they're looking at a year or so. But I have to tell you, pressing charges would be a crap shoot. The DA might not go along with it, especially in the father's case if he left the force with a good name & record. No one's eager to put away an ex-cop. And if the DA did press charges, the case might never get to trial. Both sides might agree to a plea bargain, so they could wind up with nothing more than probation & community service. But even if they didn't come to an agreement, the judge might dismiss all charges & throw the case out.*

He paused as he prepared to give me more bad news. *But if there were a trial, they'd likely win, especially if Karen testified for them. The case against them isn't strong. Another thing, it might hurt us that you didn't call the cops the same night, although we could say you were too shocked & frightened to do anything.* Tapping his fingers on the top of his enormous desk, he went on. *We'd have a better chance if we asked for a restraining order. We could also bring a civil suit against them, although I wouldn't recommend it. There's just not enough evidence.*

I ran a finger across my face. *What about the bruise?*

He shook his head. *Their lawyer would argue that we couldn't prove it came from Patrick's hitting you, & he'd be right. You could have gotten it in other ways, or it could have been self-inflicted. Besides, the bruise would be long gone before we get to court. It's not as though you sustained a serious injury with an ER chart to back it up. We'd only have photos to go on, & I don't think they'd be impressive. It's your decision, Keith, but if I were you, I'd opt for a restraining order.*

I nodded, trying to hide my disappointment. I really hoped the father & brother would go to jail. Would have served them right. Furthermore, I could undo the damage they did to me & Karen while they were still locked up. Without the 2 of them to poison her against me, we'd be back on track. Maybe we'd already be married by the time they got out.

Okay. I'll get going on it right away. He paused. *Now, uh, this is so obvious that I'm embarrassed to have to say it, but I strongly advise you against having contact with her, Keith. None at all. The last thing you want to do is give them grounds for bringing a countersuit against you. For harassment, say.*

He tried to talk to me in a comforting manner, the way an older brother might, but he wasn't very good at it. *I'm sure you're disappointed. It's obvious you care about her & that you had, uh, high hopes for the 2 of you. But sometimes things don't turn out the way we want them to.* He flashed his TV game show smile at me again. *Besides, there are millions of fish in the ocean. I'm sure you'll meet other women.*

I tried to look him in the eye but couldn't. Instead I looked at one of his splotchy pointless paintings. *I won't see her,* I said a few seconds later. *I know there are other women out there.* No use telling him that she was the only one for me, just as I was the only one for her. That we were destined for each other, with no escaping from each other. How can anyone escape from fate? That we'd heal each other's wounds. That we'd find a way to overcome all obstacles. Which is what true love is all about, isn't it? Overcoming obstacles.

Suddenly, as I sat across from him, I hated Jordan Barker. Hated this tall man with his wavy hair, who thought he was God Almighty in his $2,000 suit & silver cufflinks, holding court behind his desk the size of a picnic table. Who was *he* to keep me from my soul mate? For a moment I hated him as much as I hated the father & the brother.

I would see her again, in time. Not for days or weeks, or possibly months, but eventually. All my dreams for us would come to pass. I would see her. Jordan Barker couldn't stop me, any more than the father & the brother could. You can't defy fate.

But I didn't let Mr. Barker know I hated him. I forced myself to look friendly & respectful, & grateful for his wonderful advice. No reason to antagonize him. I might need him again, you never know.

*　　*　　*

The rest of the summer I lay low. In fact my life was almost the same as it was before we met.

I put in more hours than usual at the video place. Thirty hours per week on average, sometimes 35. The others took vacations, & the boss often asked me to fill in, so I could work as much as I wanted. Not a real demanding job, but like I said, it helped to pass the time. It also gave me the chance to bring home as many videos as I wanted, free of charge. When I wasn't working, I stayed in the apartment with Lulu & the goldfish. I cleaned & tidied up each day, vacuuming & doing the dishes & so forth, although I didn't have a lot to clean. Sometimes I watched TV or a movie I brought home. Once in a while I read the paper or a magazine. *TV Guide* & *Entertainment* were the 2 I liked most. I gave up on books when Ms. Gleiss deserted me. The only ones I had were the Bible & *Easy Family Favorites*, my mother's cookbook. I didn't use the cookbook much & I never opened the Bible.

When it wasn't too hot, I took a walk. I can't walk far, no more than half a mile, especially if it's damp. My leg starts to hurt & my limp gets worse if I try to go farther. On my worst days I can only manage a few blocks.

I wasn't seeing Karen, which didn't stop me from thinking about her. To the contrary, I thought about her more than ever. A hundred times a day I wondered where she was & what she was doing. Since I'd pretty much memorized her schedule, it wasn't hard to guess. I knew when she was at work & at home & at the Alpha. I imagined her at all those places. Waiting on customers at work, stocking shelves & writing up charge slips & so forth. Making her bed, making meals, doing laundry. Working out on the stationery bike, her muscles firm against her shorts & jersey.

Of course I knew that she was thinking of me too, wondering where *I* was & what *I* was doing.

Sometimes, not often but too often to my liking,

I imagined her with other men. I imagined them as rich & handsome. Impressive & full of themselves like Jordan Barker. I imagined her going to restaurants with them, & movies & concerts. Sometimes I imagined them kissing her good night. I even imagined them trying to take advantage of her. Trying to make her go all the way. I knew she was as lonely as I was, & for the same reason. Imagining those things hurt me terribly, not to mention it filled me with a ton of rage, but I couldn't rid my mind of them. If I ever actually saw her with another man, there's no saying what I might have done.

Sometimes I thought about her & her ex-boyfriend, John Mihaliak. I was very curious about him. What he looked like, for starters. Tall & dark, my guess was, with brooding eyes. What he did for a living, how much money he made, how he dressed, what kind of car he drove. His car—I dwelled on that, I don't know why. I imagined him in a convertible, something sporty, maybe even a Corvette. Bright red. I imagined them riding around together with the top down, his arm around her. I imagined it so vividly it made me want to puke.

Of course I wondered how he'd treated her. My hunch was that he'd hurt her, & I don't mean just once. That he'd come on to her all sweet & charming, & then he'd have a few drinks, & suddenly he wouldn't be so sweet & charming. The father & the brother had obviously treated her badly, so she probably picked a man who did the same. But she finally had enough of it & found the strength to leave him. I wondered what caused the final break. Well, I'd find out soon enough. She'd tell me. In time she'd tell me everything.

It occurred to me that I was capable of killing John Mihaliak. More than capable. If I ever had the chance, I'm pretty sure I would have. I was capable of killing anyone who hurt her.

I also spent part of each day going through the photo album.

As soon as I learned to use the Canon, I took photos of her whenever I could, up until the first time her father & brother came to my apartment. I could shoot from a distance, thanks to the zoom. The pictures were nothing special, since asking her to pose had been impossible. Just ordinary shots. Karen, as she let the cat out & back in. As she left her apartment in the morning. As she came to work, & ate lunch in the Food Court, down the corridor from her shop. As she came to the health club, carrying her gym bag on her shoulder. I'd marked down the time & date of each of them.

I'd put the photos in a dark blue leather album.

On the cover I wrote her name in stenciled letters with a bright gold magic marker. Beneath it I printed a big red heart with an arrow through it. I studied the photos until I memorized each detail of them. Before long I could tell you what she wore in each of them, what the expression on her face was like. Whether she looked happy or sad, well-rested or tired, carefree or worried.

The pictures were just a bunch of ordinary shots, but the album became my most prized possession. If a fire had broken out in my apartment & I could only grab one thing, that album would have been the one.

But, however much I thought about her (all the time!), however much I yearned for her, I took Mr. Barker's advice. I didn't write her or send presents. I went nowhere near her home or place of business. My love for her burned as bright as 1,000 candles, but I loved her from a distance. Not that I had much choice in the matter. As soon as Mr. Barker filed a restraining order against the father & brother, she filed one against me too.

One night I brought home *Casablanca* from the store. My all-time favorite movie, which I'd already seen 3 times. I'll never forget the ending, where Humphrey Bogart comes to the airport & the lovers say good-bye.

The scene where he says *At least we'll always have Paris.* I know exactly how he felt.

I don't know how it happened, but the movie triggered something in me. Made me think about the bond between soul mates. Strongest bond there is, as far as I'm concerned. The movie fed my love for her, but it made me restless too. It's not easy, loving someone from a distance, even though you know in your heart of hearts that someday you'll be together.

I had to see her again, no matter what. I wouldn't let the restraining order—which was just a piece of paper, when you think about it—stand in the way of what we had between us. Would it have stopped Humphrey Bogart from seeing Ingrid Bergman? Of course not!

I had to see her again, but where? If I went to her apartment, she might panic & call 911 before I had a chance to say a word. Same was true if I approached her in the candle shop. Besides, there'd be other people there & we needed privacy, especially after all this time apart.

Three possibilities occurred to me. I could wait for her when she went to her car in the morning, before she headed off to work. Or I could wait for her in the mall parking lot on a Thursday, the evening she worked late. Or I could wait in the back of her apartment & be there when she got home on a Thursday night. This is the one I decided on. Unlikely to find anyone else around that late. Also, as I knew from having been there, it would be easy to conceal myself. Very dark, with lots of trees & so forth. The parking lot at the mall, on the other hand, was brightly lit & security patrol cars made rounds regularly. If they found me waiting in my car, just sitting there, they might stop and ask me questions that were none of their business.

I also thought a nighttime encounter would be more romantic than a meeting in broad daylight. It would be like Humphrey meeting Ingrid at the airport.

Piece by piece, I made a plan. I'd park far away, well before I expected her, & find myself a hiding place. When she saw me, she'd be nervous, thanks to how her father & brother had poisoned her against me, but I'd reassure her, I'd let her know that she was in no danger. I'd also have a present ready, but what should it be? I went through the closet where I stored things I'd bought for her. Leather purse, gold necklace—books of poetry, CDs with love songs—all of them nice but none of them quite right. It had to be a special present for such a special moment. After all, this meeting would mark our new beginning!

I went to a different mall from the one where

Karen worked, a more expensive one on the other side of town. The mall had your typical shops, like Victoria's Secret, Sharper Image & so forth, but it had fancier ones too. I looked in windows & went inside a few, but found nothing that met with my approval. Then, when I'd almost given up, I passed a place I hadn't noticed earlier. A shop run by some museum in New York City, its windows full of all kinds of artsy-fartsy stuff, prints & posters & so forth. It was almost like a museum in its own right, or what I thought one would be like. I've never been in one myself.

I went inside. There it was, right in front of me! A statue of a cat, about a foot high, made of some shiny black material. The perfect gift.

Art has never meant too much to me, although of course I loved my paintings of Elvis & the crying clown. But you didn't have to be an expert to know that this was real classy.

The salesgirl took it off the shelf & handed it to me so I could take a closer look. The cat's face had an interesting expression. Arrogant, the way cats are. Eyes half-closed, as if someone had roused it from a nap. I liked the feel of it, smooth as a bowling ball. Heavier than I would have guessed, between 5 & 10 pounds.

Karen would be crazy about it! For a moment I

wondered if she still missed Frisky. I doubted it. People get over things.

I took out my Visa card & paid for it without a second thought, even though it cost $150. Truth is, I'd have paid twice as much.

All this happened on a Wednesday morning. I went to work at 2 that afternoon & worked straight through until 10. As luck would have it, I had the next day off. I decided on the spot that that would be the Thursday of our reunion. On Wednesday night I hardly slept, 2 or 3 hours at the most.

*　　*　　*

The tenants in Karen's building had assigned parking spaces. Karen's was near a dumpster, which sat on the edge of a vacant lot behind the building. Between the dumpster & her parking space was an oak tree. Its uppermost branches stretched above the roof of Karen's building & its trunk was broad enough for a man to hide behind. What with the tree & dumpster, you couldn't ask for better cover.

I got there just before 9:30 & hid like a tiger in the jungle. It was a bright night, no clouds, & the moon lit up a sky filled with stars. I've never known time to pass as slowly as it did that night. Each minute seemed like an hour. My heart beat like a drum, my palms turned cold & clammy. This was the most exciting moment I'd ever known. I clutched the statue of the cat for dear life, taking care not to disturb the cute red ribbon that I'd tied around its neck.

Just after 10, I heard a car pull into the driveway leading to the parking area. I peered out & saw her Honda. She parked in her space, got out, locked the car & headed for the building. It was now or never.

I came out from my hiding place & took a few steps towards her. At first she didn't hear or see me. Then she turned in my direction. We were now no more than 20 feet apart. Our eyes locked into each other's. She let out a gasp, almost a scream. *Don't be afraid, I won't hurt you,* I tried to reassure her.

You're goddamn right you won't. I didn't like her swearing. It made her sound coarse & unladylike. She also sounded very sure of herself. If she'd been frightened right after she saw me, she'd gotten over it. I wondered if she had some kind of weapon in her purse, or pepper spray or something. I also recalled that she did kick-boxing. A woman who knew how to take of herself, or so she thought.

Her eyes bore into me, her lips became a thin tight line. I yearned to see that sweet smile of hers, the one I saw that first day, in the post office. I waited for her to say something but she didn't.

I took another step toward her & held out the statue. *This is for you—*

Stay where you are. Do not, I repeat, do not come any closer. Her voice was very soft but very cold, pronouncing each word distinctly, as if she were talking to an idiot. I felt resentful, but I let it pass.

You're Keith Mueller? I nodded.

What are you doing here? I thought my father & brother made things clear.

They don't understand . . . they don't understand the way things are between us. This wasn't going as I'd planned.

She shook her head. *No. You're the one who doesn't understand. There is no us, never was & never will be.* And then she laughed! Not a happy laugh, more like a snort. *Not that a creep like you would know what to do with a woman in the first place.*

I knew it wasn't the real Karen speaking. It was the father & brother, may they rot in hell. They'd done a good job of poisoning her against me. I'd have to work hard to set things straight.

I held the statue out again, but I made no further move in her direction. *Please accept this. I know how much you care for cats.*

What's the matter? Feeling guilty over what you did to Frisky? I couldn't think of what to say.

Even in the night I saw her blue eyes widen. *Dad was right all along! You* did *do something to him, you* ____*!* I won't write what she called me but it's the worst name you can call someone & the first part of it rhymes with *clock.* It shocked me that she even knew a word like that.

She came at me & her leg flew up, quick as lightning. Her foot caught the side of my neck & part of my jaw, snapping my head back as if it were on a spring. I was still stunned when the next kick came. She'd aimed for my privates, but I twisted away from her, so it landed on my inner thigh. It didn't hurt as much as the first one but it did make me lose my balance. She was stronger than she looked, & her kicks had surprising power in them. As I staggered, trying to keep my feet beneath me, I felt her fist connect with the side of my nose. Full force. I felt blood gush across my mouth & chin in a sticky stream. Before I knew it, I was on the ground.

I've no memory of what happened next, but it's clear that something in me snapped. All the hurts &

disappointments came together & swept me up in them. The ones from my parents & sister. From my classmates & the teachers who couldn't be bothered with me & Dr. Rue with his sneaky roving hands. From Ms. Gleiss's leaving. From Karen's father & brother. And now, the final insult. Karen herself—my dearest love, my soul mate—rejecting me, attacking me.

I've no memory of what happened next, but at some point I hit her with the statue of the cat. More than once. The pathologist said her skull was broken in two places.

*   *   *

Jordan Barker was great! His fee ran over $200,000, but he was worth every penny.

He hired a shrink who spent practically a whole day with me, asking me everything about everything, from before I started kindergarten until the night of Karen's death. Then he had another shrink come in. This one was a psychologist who did all kinds of tests, asking what some inkblots meant, & to interpret a bunch of stupid pictures & so forth. Mr. Barker went over my records from the accident, all the X-rays & CT-scans & EEGs, & he had a neurologist testify about post-concussion syndrome. He had an ER doctor testify about *my* injuries the night she died (broken nose & a dislocated jaw).

He even managed to round up some character witnesses for me. Mr. Lowenstein, who ran the video store & told them what a good employee I'd been, conscientious & reliable & so forth, never causing trouble. Rev. Kresge, our minister, who'd officiated at my parents' and sister's funeral. Alvin Mueller, my first cousin, who owns a hardware store in a nearby city, the only relative I felt halfway close to. I'd planned to ask him to be best man when Karen & I got married.

At the trial, he asked the shrink all kinds of questions about my mental state. The shrink described something called *erotomania*. He said it was a real disease, as real as schizophrenia or depression, & that it caused me to do what I'd done. Then he used some gobbledygook about diminished capacity and poor ego boundaries & so forth. He struck me as someone who loved the sound of his own voice, and I didn't understand his fancy words, but that didn't matter. What mattered was that he made a good impression on the jury.

When the father & brother took the stand against me, Mr. Barker handled them perfectly. He didn't want to come down too hard on them. After all, they'd lost a family member & the jury was bound to be sympathetic. They'd take it out on me if they didn't like his cross-examination, so he pulled his punches, you could say. But he got them to admit that they broke into my apartment in an illegal fashion, & they threatened me, & they frightened me so much I'd asked for a restraining order myself. The prosecutor yapped about irrelevance, how the father & the brother weren't on trial here, but Mr. Barker said the stress they caused had contributed to my diminished capacity. I watched the jury carefully while this was going on. I knew they didn't like what they'd heard about the breaking into my apartment & so forth.

In his closing, Mr. Barker talked about the accident & how it changed me. *Traumatized me*, he said. How I lost all 3 members of my immediate family & there I was, alone in the world when just a teenager. How I'd tried to live an independent life despite my limitations. I didn't like it when he talked about my limitations, but I let it pass.

He spoke about how my actions stemmed from loneliness & love & generosity but not from malice. How hurting Karen had been the last thing I'd intended. Without quite blaming her for what happened, he pointed out how she'd attacked me first. How this tragedy might have been prevented if she hadn't been so quick to lash out at me. He described the remorse I felt about her death, which would stay with me all my life. He brought up my unblemished record, how this was my first offense of any kind, how I hadn't even gotten a speeding ticket. How I posed no danger whatsoever to society at large.

Finally, at the very end, he talked about my unhappiness, & my distorted view of the world & the people in it. About my need for treatment instead of punishment. He did everything but play the violin. A few jurors wiped their eyes.

They convicted me of manslaughter & gave me 9 years suspended after 5. It could have been much worse.

*　　*　　*

Prison's not as bad as I expected. Interesting how you can get used to things. The tiny cell, the thin mattress, the noise & lack of privacy & so forth. The food's not great but it's edible. The only thing that still bothers me a good deal is lack of privacy. I've always been a very private person.

Most guards treat us decently. You soon learn the ones who don't, & you avoid them. Some of them will even chat when they're not busy, about sports & weather & so forth.

I'm in a medium-security prison, which everyone says is a hundred times better than a maximum. I'm also in mental health housing, thanks again to Mr. Barker. It's easier to do time there, compared to general population. We see shrinks & social workers regularly, sometimes as often as once a week. In general population we're lucky if we see them twice a year.

My cellie's name is Ronald Schuster. He's older than me, 33, & he's had bad nerves since his teens. When he goes off his medication, he hears voices & believes the CIA controls his thoughts. I guess he gets pretty dangerous then, attacking the ones he thinks are out to get him. He's doing time for 1st degree assault. They have him on some new pills & he comes across as fairly normal, although he still likes to talk about the CIA. You wouldn't know he's spent most of his adult life in funny farms & prisons.

They give me medication too, to make me less depressed. Also less irritable, & less inclined to dwell on things. Can't say if it helps but Mr. Barker tells me to take it, so I do. He says it'll look good when I go before the parole board. This may sound odd but I don't feel too depressed. There's not much outside I miss.

Dr. Shah is the shrink who prescribes my medication. Conversations are brief—he's too busy to talk at length with inmates. But 2 or 3 times a month I meet with Ms. Hernandez, a social worker assigned to mental health housing. A real nice lady, about 30, thin, with brown eyes & long dark hair. Sometimes kind of hard to understand, because of her accent, but easy to talk to. She reminds me a bit of Lisa Gleiss, except that Ms. Gleiss was at least half a foot taller. Of course we talk about Karen, but we've gotten into other things. My anger, especially with my sister. My sense that I was different from everyone else, going back as far as I can remember. My fear of women—not knowing what to say to them or how to deal with them despite wanting terribly to be with one. Ms. Hernandez has tried to help me see how unrealistic I was about Karen. How I turned her into what I needed her to be.

The thing is, women have always been a mystery to me. I haven't understood them in the slightest. Well, I wouldn't go so far to say I understand them now, but at least Ms. Hernandez has made them less mysterious. She reminds me that I'll still be fairly young when I get out, & a normal relationship with a woman would still be possible.

The days & weeks & months pass slowly, but I try to keep the time filled up. I have a job, in the prison laundry, & that helps. I play cards with Ronald, gin rummy & crazy eights. He tried to teach me chess but I didn't care for it. Too complicated. Each week I take as many books & magazines as they'll give me from the library cart. Westerns & science fiction, old issues of *Readers Digest* & *Sports Illustrated*, it doesn't matter what. Funny, since I read so little before coming here.

Whenever I get the chance, I exercise. Not just when I go to rec, but in the cell as well. I shadowbox & do sit-ups & pushups. Wouldn't have expected this to happen, but I'm probably in the best shape of my life.

Ronald & I have an 18" black & white TV set in the cell. It's not the greatest but it lets us keep in touch with the world. It's his TV, so we watch what he wants. The news, & *60 Minutes* & *Entertainment Tonight* are our favorites, but we see other things. Quiz shows, sports, soap operas, whatever—you name it, we'll watch it. The soaps are kind of interesting when you get into them. Relationships between the characters are very deep.

My favorite program is the local news. Of course it's nice to know what's going on in your home town, but I'll admit that there's another reason. I've become a big fan of the woman who does the weather!

Her name is Kate Merriman. Young, not more than 25. Hard to make out her coloring from just a black & white TV, but she looks as if she's very fair. A blonde, I'm guessing, with blue eyes like Karen's, only not so close together. A perfect mouth, with fuller lips than Karen had. Now that I think about it, Karen's lips were too thin.

Kate's very smart. You can tell it from the way she talks. But you can also tell she's not stuck-up. There's something sweet & innocent about her. It comes out in her lovely, sunny smile. Even lovelier than Karen's. The thing is, Karen didn't smile much. I think about the pictures of her in my album, & almost none of them show her smiling. Kind of a sourpuss, in fact!

One night, as Kate gave the weather forecast, she smiled into the camera & I had the strangest feeling. I knew it wasn't logical, but I felt as if she were smiling straight at me. At me alone, I mean. I felt as if she knew about me somehow, even though we've never met. As if we were somehow fated to be together.

And then it dawned on me, it hit me like a load of bricks. *Kate Merriman, Keith Mueller. We had the same initials!* Tell me that's just a coincidence! All the times I've seen her, I never realized it before.

*   *   *

I've been a model prisoner. Everybody says so. All the guards, Dr. Shah, Ms. Hernandez, everybody. I've caused no trouble, never been in fights, never caught with contraband. No time in seg, no tickets. It's almost certain that I'll serve the minimum. Which means that I'll be out in 7 more months.

I plan to make a new beginning. A new job, a new apartment. New clothes—I've pretty much lived in jeans & sweatshirts, & I plan to pay more attention to the way I look. A new car, even. I guess I'm tired of the old Victoria & I'm ready for something sportier. Of course I want to get another parakeet & 2 new goldfish.

As you'd expect, there's a bunch of unanswered questions. Don't know what I'll do or where I'll live. It won't be all that easy to find myself a job, especially with a felony conviction. Plus, I'm sure there are landlords who won't be falling all over themselves to rent to me. I'll have my share of problems, but I'll work things out as I go along. Besides, I'll still have plenty of money left, even after Mr. Barker's fee.

What matters, & it's the only thing that does, is that Kate will be there with me. I'll find a way to meet her, just as I found a way to meet Karen, but this time

I'll go about it differently. I'll be smarter, more careful & more patient. When we do meet, she'll fall in love with me, just as I've already fallen in love with her, & she & I will become as One. One in spirit, one in body, always. We'll become a world unto ourselves.

It took more pain than I care to remember, & all kinds of hard experience, including years in prison, to make me understand this, but I do now—a man can have 2 soul mates in a lifetime. Or 3, or maybe even more.

#

AUTHOR'S NOTE

FOR MORE THAN TWENTY YEARS *I practiced psychiatry in a variety of correctional settings: prisons, jails, and facilities for the criminally insane. The clientele included teenagers and old men, creators of ruckuses in donut shops and serial killers, inner-city gangbangers and possessors of postgraduate degrees. Some had IQs that would have qualified them for Mensa, and others thought Jimmy Carter was still in the White House. Some were incarcerated for a few days, others were lifers, and a few were on Death Row.*

A mixed blessing, the opportunity to have done such work. On the one hand, the setting is bleak, intimidating, and undeniably dangerous. To get there you may have to traverse up to four sets of locked doors—that is, once you've made it past a fence topped with razor wire. Vigilance is a constant necessity, and it soon becomes part and parcel of your mindset. You learn the obvious (always sit between the inmate and office door) and the less obvious (keep a heavy stapler out of the inmate's reach; he could fracture your skull with it). A patient's desire to make positive changes in his life, a sine qua non *for successful treatment outcomes, is frequently slim to nil. But if an inmate-patient does desire it, the cards are often stacked against him. His day-to-day caretakers may despise him and dedicate themselves to making his sentence as miserable as possible (admittedly, others will try to help him). It may be decades before he's free, and even then he may lack the most basic job skills or community supports. Recidivism rates are high throughout the system.*

The work is draining and exhausting if you take it seriously. And the numbers are against you. As the population of the incarcerated has swelled—about 1.3 million in the United States, as of this writing—the ratio of inmates to mental health staff is overwhelming. The potential for burnout is enormous.

On the other hand, you can be useful, at times, to a point. You can listen to those who've rarely been listened to; you can show compassion toward those who have no experience with it. You can prescribe medications to alleviate depression, to address hallucinations and para-